Al-agaila

The Camp of Suffering:
A Boy's Tale

Ali Hussein

ORIGINAL WRITING

ISBNS
PARENT : 978-1-78237-674-3
EPUB: 978-1-78237-675-0
MOBI: 978-1-78237-676-7
PDF: 978-1-78237-677-4

A CIP catalogue for this book is available from the National Library.

Published by ORIGINAL WRITING LTD., Dublin, 2014.

Printed by CLONDALKIN GROUP, Glasnevin, Dublin 11

To Sofyan

إلى أسية جو
مع كامل أحترامي
وتقديري ٮ
أرجو أن ٮنال أعجابك
لوكٮٮٮع عليٮٮ

23/5/2015

Contents

INTRODUCTION

"In 1884 Libya was the last "Welaya" State belonging to the Ottoman Empire in North Africa as Egypt was colonized by the British. Tunisia, Morocco and Algeria were under the direct rule of the French. The increased weakening of the Ottoman Empire had left Libya suffering from diseases and lacking in any medical and educational centres. There were only 5,000 Turkish soldiers in the whole state. This caused the surfacing of a religious and political movement. It's goals were to educate and fight the inequity imposed by the rule of the "Waly"- the governor of the state under the direct orders of the Sultan of the Empire in Istanbul. The leader of this movement was a man called Mohammed Ben Ali Al-Sonussi, who later became very formidable political voice of the Libyans for their struggle against the Italian invasion. He began building Al Zawaya – Islamic centres and lodges across the country and all the way to Sudan and Chad. Before his death he gave the leadership of the "Alsanoussia Method" to Ahmed Al Shareef Al-Sonussi which he led by the example of his predecessor and the "order" began gathering followers across Libya. Alsanoussia was more like a fraternity or brotherhood but not a sect. The 150,000 Bedouins out of 200,000 (which was the population of Cyrenaica) were nomads, but all were followers of Alsanoussia. At the same time destiny was preparing another man, whose name would later be written in the history books as the "Lion of the Desert" and "The Sheik of Al-Mujahideen", the hero who led the struggle against the Italians until he met his fate by the hands of a brutal man who was hailed by the "Il Duce" as the "Pacifier of Libya" and "the Butcher of Fezzan" by Libyans. The hero named Omar Al-Mukhtar and the villain was General Rodolfo Graziani who went on to become the Vice Governor of Libya and the Military Governor of Cyrenaica.

Omar Al-Mukhtar was born in 1862 in the region of Al Jabal–Alakhdar - the Green Mountain in the eastern part of Libya and from a very young age his father sent him to Zawya Janzour, one of the Islamic centres built by Sidi Ahmed Al Shareef. There he learned Arabic and the teachings of Islam and completed the recitation of the Holy Quran by heart.

His father fell ill during his pilgrimage to Mecca and before he died he gave his last will to one of his closest companions to take care of Omar's education and his well-being. The man, upon his return, fulfilled the promise and the deed was done. Omar Al-Mukhtar was sent to the Zawyat Al Jagboub in the Libyan Sahara Desert. There he met his mentor and the man who raised him to be the leader of the Mujahideen. Omar met Sidi Ahmed Al Shareef. When he was 16 years old. Omar Al-Mukhtar dedicated eight years of study at Zawya Jagboub before he went to earn his living after having a family. Sidi Ahmed Al Shareef appointed Omar as the Sheik of Zawya Alkousor in the Green Mountain. Omar kept close with Sidi Ahmed Al Shareef and fought bravely against the French in Chad and the English in Sudan. Al-Mukhtar was born a natural warrior, his travelling with Sidi Ahmed made him an expert guide of the desert, Sahara roads and made him form great relationships with chiefs of the Libyan tribes in Cyrenaica and the desert region of Fezzan. Later he formed great allies with the Egyptian Revolutionary leaders in their struggle against the British. All this helped Omar to be a military leader and he would soon engage in a long 20–year guerrilla–style war against the fascists. His strong character and oration made people listen to him every time he spoke and later his executioner - Marshall Graziani wrote, "he was truly a brave man who loved his religion and country".

In September 1911 Italy declared war against the Ottomans and said Italy would take Libya. On the 3rd of October 1911 Italy began an invasion of Libyan coastal cities by sea and air. Tens of thousands of soldiers landed on Libyan soil. The Libyans revolted and engaged in fierce battles with the Italians. Despite the Libyans fighting bravely, the Ottomans signed the Treaty of Lausanne in 1912 in which they handed over Libya to the Italians. Now the Libyans felt let down by the Ottomans, who had ruled them for hundreds of years under the banners of Islam. The Libyans were now left to face one of the emerging powers in the 20th century alone."

* * *

CHAPTER ONE

Dublin, 2009

My heart pounded as I experienced yet another nightmare. I heard the screaming of a young girl as she was being carried away by soldiers, and her mother crying. Then it switched to me being interrogated, being slapped and punched, while men were shouting at me as I lay on the ground, bleeding. And it culminated in me seeing my father walk into a black abyss, smiling one last time before being engulfed in a dark greyish cloud of smoke. I called out to him before he disappeared, but he never heard me. I screamed before opening my eyes, realising it was just another dream but what did it mean? Some of the events were from my father's, but what troubled me was my father walking into that black infinite mass of nothingness and then disappearing forever.

I decided a cold shower was in order and that maybe would banish these ominous thoughts. I dried myself and got dressed, but still a foreboding hung over me like a dark rain cloud. I ran downstairs and switched on the gas cooker and began making Arabic coffee. It is brewed with cardamom. My family always send me enough supplies because they know how much I love it. I put some music on and the unmistakable, angelic voice of Fayruoz began singing my favourite song "*Shadi.*" It is about a little boy who loved a girl from a neighbouring tribe and they used to meet and play in the mountain of Aldrouz in Lebanon. A war broke out and Shadi never made it to see his girl but she went every winter all her life, hoping that Shadi would appear through the cedar trees.

The aroma of my Arabic coffee filled the room. I sat down at the kitchen table and puffed on my cigarette in between taking sips from my cup, which was specially designed for this particular coffee. But the weirdest thing was that the minute I tasted it, it took me back 20 years earlier when I lived in Libya. It took me to the event of that day, which will remain with me as long as I live. It was 7 o'clock in the morning that day and it was a typical day for a family of 11 children. There was a lot of buzz and movement. Some of us were sitting at the breakfast table, some were getting dressed and others were looking for their school bags. I was in no hurry as my first lecture started at 10 o'clock, so decided to have breakfast. I kissed Mum's hand and her forehead and did the same with my father before I sat beside him. He was as usual fully dressed and immaculate.

"How are you, Khalid?" he asked while making different piles of money for our weekly spending.

"All good, dad," I replied while taking my coffee from my mother's hand. She was busy making sure that everyone got their breakfast and she always had pots of tea, coffee and hot milk at the breakfast table, as we each had our own preferred morning drink.

"Why up so early? I thought you don't have to be at the university until 10 o'clock," Mum asked while sending Souad to the kitchen to bring more khak and greyba – it is a traditional morning sweets.

"Yes, that's right, Mum, but something woke me up. I feel like I've been saddened by something or someone, but I can't explain what."

"I seek refuge with the Lord from the evil things," Mum responded very quickly. "Just read some verses from the Quran when you perform your morning prayer. That will put your heart at ease."

"Yes I will," I replied and then turned my attention to my father. "Yes, everything's fine at university."

Shukri grabbed his briefcase from under his seat. He pushed up his glasses with his index finger and said that he would not be home for lunch as he was going to stay late in his office to study a court case which he had to attend the next morning. Shukri is the eldest and always busy reading, he is very successful lawyer.

Mum followed him all the way to the door. "God protect you, son. Take good care of yourself," Mum said before returning to the breakfast table to make sure that everything was running smoothly.

The honking of the bus horn outside alerted Samia and Aml, It was the company bus that took them to where they worked as secretaries. They grabbed their handbags, kissed my mother and ran toward the door.

"Hatim, Anees, your friends are outside," Samia shouted.

"Okay," Hatim yelled back. "Tell them we'll be out in couple of minutes." They were high school students and they loved walking just to check out the girls on the way to school.

"Come on, get going, boys. Don't let the lads wait. Take your money," my father said in his deep, husky voice.

"Okay, we are leaving, Mum." They picked up their money from the edge of the table and left.

"Where is Adel?" Mum asked.

"I think he is in his room getting ready."

Adel was a year younger than me. We hung around together when we had time. He was a good brother and fun to be with. Adel and I did everything together as young children. We used to go to my aunty in the countryside every summer. The fun was always mighty as we formed friendship with all the local children over the years. We spent almost the whole of our summer holidays there.

My mother must have called my name at least twice before I responded. "Are you okay, Son?" she asked as she handed me my breakfast.

"I'm fine. I just daydreamed for a moment, Mum." Adel came out of his room and greeted everyone again. He put his empty cup of coffee on the table and took out his car keys from his pocket and asked me if I wanted a lift.

"Thanks, Adel. I'm not starting my first lecture until 10 o'clock, so you go ahead. I shall see you later this evening. Maybe we will watch a movie together or go and visit some friends."

"Okay then," Adel replied before he turned around to our parents. "Have a good day. Do you need anything, Mum? I can bring something on the way home from work."

"No, son, you go ahead," she told him.

Dad then spoke. "I will finish early today. I will go to the city market and get everything. I feel like having seafood again."

"Lovely," Adel said with a big smile, "All right, then, I am leaving."

My father loved seafood. He would have eaten it every day of the week. But to his credit he always helped out in the kitchen to cook the food as he was an expert in making different dishes with the greatest sauces. The man had us hooked on it from a very young age and he did it just to tease Mum.

"All right, son. What's happening lately in the university?" my father asked.

"Everything's good. Nothing to worry about, Dad," I assured him.

My mother stepped in and said, "You have to listen to your father carefully, son."

I nodded and listened.

"It's a difficult time as you know in the university, and the month of April can bring confrontation between the students and the revolutionary committee," my father explained.

"I know that, Dad, but there's nothing to worry about. I don't get involved in any political argument with them. I'm just committed to my study."

"Very well. Make sure that your friends aren't involved. I just fear for you, Khalid." My father's words were laced with anxiety.

"Believe me, Dad, all the lads are the same. We never speak about any political issues with anyone we don't know."

"That's it, that's exactly what I am talking about, you can't trust anyone these days. Do you understand?" Dad emphasised his point strongly.

"Yes, Dad. I agree with you. but I grew up with these guys, so I know them like I know you and they're very responsible, none of us will do anything silly to put any of us in danger. "

"You're not getting the point, son. You shouldn't discus any political views with *anyone*. Period!" my father repeated himself.

"Fair enough, Dad, I promise I won't get involved in any of that," I said.

"Thank's, son. Now you put our hearts at ease and I can go to work without having to worry all day." My father stood up and told Mum that he would be home a bit earlier because he wanted to help her cook the fish. Dad took out his silver pocket watch from his waistcoat pocket. Then he opened it with the same hand, nodded his head and said, "Come on, Khalid, walk me to the car."

"Sure, Dad." I followed him like a soldier following his leader. As we got to the car he looked at me with a face full of love. "Son, I am getting older and I can't afford to lose any of you in circumstances like that. Be good and take good care of yourself." He took my hand and put a lot of money into my palm.

I kissed his hand and said, "God bless you and may Allah protect you." I stood there until his car disappeared out of view. I went straight back into the house. I started helping my mother clearing the table. We chatted and then I told her that I must start getting ready for college.

I went to the bathroom and had a quick shower. As the hot water sprayed onto my face, I began to think of father's words to me. Some inner voice warned me that something was going to happen. I got out of the shower and headed into my room to get dressed and to prepare the books and notes that I had to bring with me. As I returned to the sitting room, my mother had already commenced her housework with the radio still playing patriotic songs. These songs were very boring, so I looked for a different station and I found one- the "Voice of Cairo", more to the point, the voice of Umo Kalthoum – the most famous singer in the Arab world. She was singing "Enta Omri" -"You Are My Life".

My thoughts returned to my father again and I began thinking about all the stories he told me. He was the most extraordinary man I had ever known. He told me everything, as I was the one who always accompanied him wherever he went. Dad told me stories that he never told anyone else and this allowed me to know him better with the exception of my mother, of course. His stories were of agony, pain, misfortune, betrayal and indignation and how he emerged from all these hopeful, successful and with no regrets. I understood him well when he talked to us because he knew the price that you had to pay in a world full of hate. Father never gave up hope and he understood the concept of loss and gain because he had experienced it. I knew why my father wanted a big family and lots of kids around him because he knew what it is like to have no brother or sister to be there for you when you need them to comfort you in a time of sorrow. My dad understood the value and the price of everything.

All my life I understood well why my mother loved him more than any other woman loved her husband I think simply because she lived and felt his pain so closely. I now understand the fears that he had for us because he knew the meaning of loss and for a man who lived the life he had, not once did he reprimand or punish us during his entire life as a parent. My father made everybody around him laugh and always gave without asking for anything in return. The most amazing thing was that I never heard him giving examples from his own experience in life to us when we needed advice. He never said much but you knew exactly what he wanted by looking at your eyes. His greatest moments of joy were when we all sat together having dinner or lunch. He just smiled with his eyes almost welling, as I knew he remembered those days when he was a little boy. My father spoke four languages and recited the Quran by heart. Dad loved listening to classical Italian opera. He loved to dress in suits and smoked the pipe and cigars.

When I left home to resume my studies abroad, he did not say much but he gave me his watch and the Holy Quran, his own copy that he had from an early age of his life, which I still have to this day. I think he was trying to say that time is the greatest weapon if you use it right and God is the one you must seek in the moments of despair. Faith and time, those got my father through the days of indignation, and he emerged victorious.

But deep down I couldn't shake off the feeling that something bad was going to happen at the university later that day and unfortunately for me and many other students, my instincts would prove correct and nothing but horror and terror awaited me.

CHAPTER TWO

When Mum called my name, it distracted me from some deep pondering. My friend Fawsi had arrived to take me to the university. I invited him in for a cup of coffee but he declined as we had to pick up our other friends. I kissed my mother good-bye.

Mum smiled and said, "Don't forget what your father told you, to take good care of yourself."

"Yes, Mum, I will," I replied and departed. Fawzi was waiting in the car and as soon as I got into it, he put his foot on the accelerator.

"Who are we going to pick up first?" I enquired.

"Probably Anees and then Majdi."

"What about Nabeel?"

"Ah, Nabeel phoned me this morning, He said he won't be going with us."

"Did you do anything exciting last night?

Fawzi sighed before answering, "Ah, not really. My uncle came visiting from the country with his family so we kind of hung around with them. They stayed the night. I think they're leaving today."

I had known these lads since the early days of secondary school and we got to know each other more when we used to organise football matches. Even though we went to different high schools the football matches became more official as we had a high school league. We became best friends as the days went by. We got to know each others' families and the five of us were like real brothers. During the final exams we claimed a room at my home and we turned it into a study room. Mum and my sisters worked almost around the clock supplying us with food, coffee, tea and small snacks. We always passed the exams with high marks.

But things changed when we got to university and that's why our fathers were very concerned for our safety, as gathering in groups and in regular times in Libya in those days would attract the attention of the revolutionary committees students. Even though we spoke of reforms and freedom of speech in the university, we only did it amongst ourselves We were young university students and fear was the last thing on our minds. We did ease off a bit in meeting and hanging around on a daily basis.

Soon we were outside Anees' house and we collected him.

As the car drove over the bridge to take the airport road toward Majdi's house, we engaged in a full conversation. The tall frame of Majdi appeared to us from a distance, as he waited in the corner of his street with a cigarette in his mouth. He took three or four drags from his cigarette, almost squeezing the life out of it, before he jumped in with a big smile on his face.

After arriving at the main gates, we noticed something unusual. Lots of cars were moving very slowly ahead of us. There were lots of army personnel holding their automatic machine guns and I could tell by the way they held them that they were ready to fire at any time. There were also many revolutionary committee students in their civilian clothes but armed.

"What's going on?" I asked

"I do not know" Fowzi replied.

"What do you think, guys? Should we turn back and leave?" Majdi suggested.

"That will be a very foolish move as it will draw their attention to us and become suspicious, I explained.

The revolutionary students were checking the passengers of every car and asking for student identification.

As our car reached the gate, we lowered the windows almost simultaneously. Two revolutionary committee students flanked our car from both sides and asked for ID, lowering their heads to examining us.

"What's happening this morning?" I asked while we handed over our student passes.

He gave me back my ID and replied, "You'll find out for yourself. Now keep moving."

Fawzi drove away slowly. There were few minutes of silence between us until Anees broke it.

"We are here now. We'll find out sooner or later." We arrived at the huge car park that was situated just below the main hall. It had long, high marble steps. We parked the car after few minutes as there were lots of cars trying to get parking spaces. We walked toward the steps and as we reached the last step we saw something that sent shivers down our spines - a gallows and a rope with a noose dangling from the middle.

"Someone is going to be hanged," I mumbled. Not a word passed between us as we looked at one another with concern. There was no time for talking. The library was to our right and the big student canteen was facing us along with lots of corridors that led to different faculties.

Soldiers positioned themselves on top of every building. They were also armed with GPMGs (General Purpose Machine Guns) and bazookas. This was definitely not going to be a normal school day. There were hundreds of students gathering in small groups, but no one was safe here and the question that was on everyone's mind - who, or how many, were going to be hanged? There were students coming from every direction led by the revolutionary committee. They were raising their guns in the air and shouting revolutionary chants, "death to the traitors". The atmosphere was so tense and gloomy, everyone seemed to be lost and on edge. Consternation had crept into some students and they began panicking, and in order to overcome their fears they chanted with the revolutionary committee members.

A few minutes later the chanting grew louder and closer, with more people joining in. Suddenly about 15 or 20 of the revolutionary committee students appeared from behind the library building, pulling and roughly handling a man in shabby black clothes with his head completely covered with a black hood and a sash across his shoulders. "Traitor" was written across the sash in white paint. They were looking everywhere, trying to encourage the students to chant with them. The student was walking to his fate but could not see what was going on around him.

"That must be terrible," I said. He followed every move they wanted him to make and never resisted or fell. He was so quiet and calm despite their manhandling.

They reached the gallows and he did not move, standing tall but hopeless. They looked at us with eyes full of anger and wanted to make an example of this man. It was clear that if anyone tried to be a hero or mess with the principles of the revolution, then he or she would suffer the same fate. The noose was placed around the student's neck and was tightened. I saw Nabeel coming up the stairs and it looked like he already heard that someone was going to be hanged. He spotted us and moved toward where we stood and did not say a word.

The shouting and tension increased and reached frenzied level. In one crazy moment, they pulled the lever and the trap door underneath the man's feet opened. He dropped with no movement and my heart dropped also. I looked around, all the faces were ashen. I felt like the whole universe started reeling. I wanted to save him and even imagined how to do it, but there was no room for bravery, as one move from any of the students could end in a mass killing. Then something horrible occurred. Even the most imaginative mind would not dare to think it. They held his waist and legs tightly and pulled him down amongst some kind of hysteria with roaring and screaming. It was the most barbaric thing I had ever witnessed.

The shouting and screaming became louder and one by one girls unable to take any more began fainting. Lila was very close to me and we had an attraction for each another. She collapsed and became unconscious. Without thinking I went straight to her. I thought that was the normal thing to do when someone needed help, at least in this particular situation. I held her head in my arms and started calling her name with my right hand tapping her cheek in a desperate attempt to resuscitate her.

Suddenly everything went black. I felt like someone had just hit me on the head with a rock. Someone pulled my hair and I felt like I was being scalped. Others were kicking me and then I was dragged like an animal for about 20 metres before I found my feet and managed to stand after a great struggle. They punched me and shouted, "bloody traitor", "sympathiser", "bring him to Al Mathaba". This was the revolutionary committee's headquarters in the university. They pushed me inside the room and asked me to sit on a chair. I was surrounded and their eyes were full of contempt.

"Who is she? How do you know her?" one asked while yanking my hair.

"She is a friend of mine. She goes to the same faculty I attend."

"Do you know that guy we just hung?" another one asked.

"No I don't," I replied.

"Why did you do that, you fucking bastard?"

"I was just trying to help her, that's all," I said, desperately trying to avoid another beating.

"You don't do nothing, you just watch! Are you trying to be a hero? You're nothing but scum, do you hear?"

This was an interrogation and no matter what you said or wanted to say, it was going to be the wrong thing anyway. The best tactic was to remain silent and answer with as little as possible.

"We will hang you from your legs like a sheep if you ever do something like that again!" screamed another. I felt so angry and wanted to hit back and tell them that they were the scum, but deep down I knew that it would only give them an excuse. My father's advice that he gave me this morning and his face were the only things I could hear and see now.

A few seconds later another one entered the room and shouted, "Come on, we need you out there. Let's go, let's go!"

I was saved only by the act of God and the prayers of my parents. One of them pulled me and said that if I ever tried to be a big guy again, they would squash me and then pushed me toward the door. As I turned, they all kicked me one after another. Despite being bruised everywhere, I did not feel any pain.

As I was walking through the corridor I felt empty, humiliated, drained and totally dejected. My face bore a sad and sorrowful expression as my soul was broken. Upon returning to the hall the body of that student was still dangling. Most of the students had left. The lads were waiting for me and I could see the relief and happiness on their faces when they saw me. They all patted me on the shoulder. In some bizarre way it was like saying that you had done well.

Fawzi gave me a lift back to my house. We stayed quiet for the whole journey. When I walked in Mom and my sisters were dressing the table for lunch. They all paused for a second and looked at me with eyes full of surprise and horror. I know they wanted to say sorry. They knew about the hanging, but I never mentioned the unfortunate incident that I was involved in.

Having briefly greeted them, I went to my room and stayed there for the whole day. The next morning I woke up so bruised and battered. I met Lila and we took a quiet table at the library. Lila spoke so softly.

"You were so brave to do that. Thank you, Khalid. I told my father about you."

"Thanks, Lila, but there's something I'd like to talk to you about. After that incident, I can't trust them. I'm not sure that I will remain here. I think I'll take the first opportunity to leave the country," I explained, knowing that it would sadden her.

"But you know, Khalid, that I..."

"Yes I know, me too. You have to understand, Lila, and believe me it's so hard for me, but I have to go and it will be for a long time."

Lila's tears started falling, but deep down she knew it was better for me to go. She also knew that I would be much safer abroad, as these guys would now keep a close eye on me.

Soon we started looking at every opportunity to study abroad. I was the lucky one as I got that chance and my parents were first to look favourably on the decision. Two days before leaving the country, I went to the university for the last time. I met with Lila and we walked and talked for hours, and then had coffee in the student canteen.

"I will miss you, Khalid. You know that you'll always be in my heart. I will pray for you," Lila said softly. I could see that she battled to hold back the tears.

"I'll miss you too, Lila. You take good care of yourself."

Lila walked me to the car and we said farewell with tears streaming down her cheeks. That was the last time I saw Lila, and many a times I thought about what might have happened if I had stayed. The hanging of students soon spread across the country in every university and faculty.

The farewell was painful and sad. My father brought me early that morning to the airport and before entering the security check, I hugged him and it seemed like neither of us wanted to let go.

"You take good care of yourself, my son. Focus on your studies, and if you ever need anything, you know I'm here for you?"

"Don't worry. I won't let you down, Dad," I said with as much assurance as I could muster.

When I finally let go, I saw tears in his eyes for the first time ever, and that was the last time I saw my father. Two months later I received a phone call from Anees. He was in Argentina. Following political unrest, many students were taken for interrogation. Majdi and Nabeel were among the first to be taken. It took the revolutionary committee days to find Fawzi as he was hiding in a tank of water in the roof of his house for five full days and when his family eventually managed to take him out of the tank, he was white like a ghost and on the brink of death.

Few days later, he was arrested and the interrogation lasted two full years for the three of them before they were released. The five of us living abroad now, in different parts of the world and after 20 years, we moved on with our lives. We all have families and we kept in touch, but never spoke of the horrific memories of those days as it left deep wounds in our hearts and scars on our souls. Sometimes those visions still haunt me both day and night, and cry for the mothers of those who lost their lives only for one reason, that they voiced their opinion for freedom and reforms.

* * *

A combination of Fayruoz's singing and the aroma of my cardamom coffee snapped me out of my reverie. The clouds of cigarette smoke wafted slowly toward the half–opened kitchen window. Relentless rain lashed down and that sinister feeling lingered. I made myself another cup of coffee and the phone started ringing. I ran into the sitting room and picked it up.

"Hello?"

"Hi, Khalid, it's me, Fathi."

"Hi, Fathi, how are you?

"I'm good. Is everything okay with you?"

"Yes, everything's okay. I'm not up to much really, just hanging around. What's the weather like at your end? The rain is hammering down here."

"Did you hear anything from back home?"

"Well I was talking to them three days ago and they're all in good form. Everything seemed to be all right."

"So you didn't hear from anyone this morning?"

"No, nothing." I was beginning to get a little worried. "Why? Is there something I should know?"

"No, not really. Listen I will give you a buzz later on. Take care."

"All right then, I will talk to you soon." I put down the phone and my worries started escalating as I thought the conversation was a bit weird, and I thought he was trying to see if I knew about something, or he knew something but he decided not to tell me.

I sat on the couch for a while, contemplating this turn of events, then I picked up the phone and I dialled the number for my house back home. After punching in the number, it rang for a while, but I could not get through. I repeated this a few times and then finally someone picked up the phone.

"Hello."

"Yes, who is that? I can't hear you. There is a lot of noise in the background."

"It's me, Khalid."

"What do you want?"

There was something wrong here. Normally when I phoned home they would be glad to hear from me but this time they asked me, "What do you want?" in an unkind manner. Something was wrong indeed! I kind of recognised the voice, but it did not belong to any member of my family.

"It's Khalid," I repeated. "Can I speak to my mother?" It was silent for few seconds and then the voice of my brother, Shukri, came on, but he sounded rather drained and sad. He talked for a few moments. He told me that our father has passed away. I was listening and tears ran down my cheeks. It felt like my heart was going to stop. My head reeled and the room began spinning. I put down the receiver and did not know what to do. I was lost.

Maybe some fresh air might do me some good, I thought. After putting on my coat and scarf, I grabbed my keys and ran out the house, closing the door behind me. Fayruoz's voice was still in my head singing, "Twenty years the snow has come and gone, but Shadi hasn't returned."

The rain ceased and the skies cleared a bit. So many thoughts were swimming around in my head and my heart was filled with different emotions. I was talking to myself and the tears just kept streaming down. I knew something was going to happen, but I was not expecting it to be that big.

I reached the village and without thinking, I was at my favourite place, the bench by the lighthouse on the coast road facing the great ocean. This was my minaret, my place of solitude where I spoke to the sea and shed tears for the people I left behind long ago or when I cried for the inequity shown towards people. Having sat down, I lit my cigarette and took a long drag on it while gazing at the big ocean, all I saw were pictures flashing before my eyes of faces, places and memories of a happier time. . All I can hear now the voice of my father whispering softly in my ear telling me his story, as he did when I was very young long ago.

CHAPTER THREE

Above Al Koufra, the sun hung in an azure sky on one afternoon in the month of October 1911. The resting place for the trading caravans going to Africa, and it was the stronghold city for Al-Sonussi in the heart of the Libyan Sahara Desert. The leaders of the Sonousian movement were in Zawyat Al Koufra along with Omar Al-Mukhtar. He was in Al-Koufra conducting business with the Grand Sonousi, Sidi Ahmed Al-Shareef. They were taking shelter from the beating sun by the wall of Al-Zaweya among other leaders of the Al-Sonussia movement and the leaders of the Sahara tribes, drinking the traditional afternoon tea, which followed the big lunch, as it is the main meal of the day. They were discussing the deployment of more men to fight alongside their brothers in nearby Sudan against the British and to Chad against the French. Suddenly, an image appeared in the horizon, and it looked like dancing smoke on water by the effect of the mirage. One man stood and put his right hand over his eyebrow to block out the sun's rays trying to identify it.

"We have a visitor, Sidi Ahmed. Look, he is definitely coming towards Al-Zaweya,, A horseman" the man shouted with excitement. They all put their hands over their eyes trying to spot the horseman.

Sidi Omar stood and said, "Whoever the horseman is, he's very welcome. I just hope he's bringing good news. He seems to be in a hurry to get here."

The sound of the galloping horse became louder as he got closer.

"He looks like he's from Barka!" a man yelled as he recognised the outfit of the people of that region. Soon the horse came to a halt. One man rushed forward and got hold of the horse.

"Mrhaba, Mrhaba," the man saluted.

"Assalamu Alaikum," the Stranger said while he was jumping from the saddle, rushing toward Sidi Ahmed, the Grand Sonousi, and he kissed his hand as it was a Libyan tradition, a mark of respect toward the elderly and for noble people, and especially for parents.

"May God bless your soul, son. You are very welcome," Sidi Ahmed said. Then the man embraced Sidi Omar and saluted all the men in that gathering.

"Sit down. It must have been a hard and long journey for you," Sidi Ahmed added while another man handed him Al-Jarra. This is like a jug made of clay and it keeps the water fresh and cold when it is placed in the shade. The stranger took a mouthful from it.

"Saha, Saha!" all the men shouted.

"Massoud, go and ask the ladies to prepare some food for our guest," Sidi Ahmed ordered.

"At once, Sidi Ahmed," the man replied before running to the nearby house.

"How are you, and how's Barka?" Sidi Omar asked.

"I am afraid, gentlemen, that I have some bad news for you," the stranger answered in a sad voice.

"Speak nothing for now. You must have your food first," insisted Sidi Ahmed, as it was a Libyan tradition that the messenger should not deliver his message until he was fed and recovered from his journey.

A few minutes elapsed and a man put a big dish of traditional couscous made with lamb and vegetables in front of the guest and encouraged him to eat. He was very hungry as he devoured a big share of the dish before he lifted the Al-Jarra to wash down the meal.

"Alhamdulillah. Thank you, gentlemen, that was delicious."

"Saha, Saha," all the men replied.

"Haya ya, Massoud, start making another round of tea," one young Sonousi asked.

"Now Abdulhmid, speak. We're all ears and anxious to hear the news from Barka," Sidi Omar politely asked.

"As I said, gentlemen, it's rather bad news. As a matter of fact, it's a total catastrophe."

"Speak in heaven's name; our hearts are in our mouths!" urged Sidi Ahmed.

"Well, I don't really know how to begin and where to start, but our home, our country has been invaded," the man answered nervously.

"What? Are you saying that Libya has been invaded by another country?" Sidi Omar asked in an astonished manner.

"That's exactly what I meant, Sidi Omar."

"But by whom?" one Sonousi asked.

"By the Italians."

"This is truly devastating news, but how and when?" Sidi Ahmed enquired with a grim expression.

"Well, it all happened in the beginning of this month, when the news came that the Italians had launched an assault on the coastal cities and that Tripoli, Derna and Tobrouk have been taken after a revolt by the men of those cities. The news came that their fleet are moving toward Benghazi and that's why I am here, gentlemen. After an emergency meeting by all the chiefs of all the tribes of the Green Mountain and the leading members of the city of Benghazi, it was decided that I come to Al Koufra to bring the information to you, Sidi Omar. People really need you to be there in this difficult time. You're the only one who can unite and lead them."

"You have done really well, my son. May Allah bless your soul," Sidi Ahmed said. He then pointed at three young men: Kkalifa, Massoud and Ebraheem.

"Yes, Sidi Ahmed," they all replied in unison.

"Go at once and inform all the men of the city of Al Koufra and the nearby villages and the peole of the oases to attend the emergency meeting in the mosque after the Maghreb prayer and all must attend."

At the meeting, all the leaders of Alsanoussia pledged their allegiance to the Grand Sonousi to do what God had asked them to do in circumstances like this: to defend their country and vow to fight behind their leader. Sidi Ahmed appointed Sidi Omar to go back to the green mountain and prepare the men for holy war against the invaders.

By the break of dawn, Sidi Omar Al-Mukhtar and the messenger were leading voluntary horsemen and camel–caravans of supplies and arms. They were heading toward the Green Mountain. Sidi Ahmed and the people of Al Koufra, young and old, men and women, were standing in huge numbers to bid them farewell. They stood there until the caravan disappeared behind the palm trees in the outskirts of Al Koufra.

CHAPTER FOUR

Clouds were enveloping the skies above the city of Benghazi, threatening rain. The small city dreaded winter, as it turned its sandy streets into mud and flooded their houses. But in that winter of 1911, something else had kept the locals awake for days. It was the waiting for the Italian fleet to appear on its shores, after learning that Tripoli, Derna and Tobrouk had been attacked and the Italians were moving toward their city. The fear of the invasion left people with many sleepless nights. They knew that the Ottomans had a weak army of approximately 5,000 soldiers spread around the huge country of Libya. The feeling among the locals was like someone being sentenced to death and waiting for the time of the execution. Young men of the city patrolled its beaches day and night to see if the Italians' fleet would appear on the horizon. Nothing been sighted yet, but it was only a matter of time.

The Turkish officers, the governor of Benghazi, the mayor and the leading men of the city were meeting day and night, contemplating how the situation can be approached.

"We will start building bunkers around the city. We will train and arm everyone who can fight, and seek all the help we can get from the villagers. We will not give them any chance to land," one Turkish officer insisted.

"What about if we evacuate all women and children from the city first?" the governor added.

"No, we need our women and children to be with us. It will give us something to fight for," a leading man argued.

"I think we should raise the white flag, tricking them into thinking that the city is surrendering, to prevent the shelling of Benghazi and when they land, we will take them by surprise," the mayor suggested. There were so many ideas, and the men argued and debated, and sometimes were shouting or screaming at each other, but finally agreeing on one thing, that the city should fight and never surrender. The small Christian community decided to seek shelter in the Catholic Church and wait for the outcome.

Officers began training every man that could fight and the volunteers started coming to the city from every corner of the countryside. They decided to meet the Italians at the Altamaha Beach as it was rich with palm trees. Many thought here where the Italians would land their troops, as it will provide their soldiers with cover.

In the evening of 18 October 1911, the Italian armada appeared on the horizon and slowly sailed toward the city. Once they took their position facing Benghazi, the order was given to anchor. The fleet consisted of two gunships, seven frigates, and troop carriers with 5,000 soldiers. The inhabitants waited anxiously for the Italians' next move.

After couple of hours, the advance naval party for negotiating had docked in the harbour, carrying on board an officer and few navy personnel. The boat was well received by the mayor of Benghazi, the Catholic priest and few national and Turkish officers among some other leading men of the city. They were holding lanterns and had some water and bread as a gesture of hospitality. However, the Italians were not so benevolent. The officer wasted no time and handed a letter to the mayor before he sailed back to his ship.

* * *

Upon Sidi Omar's return from Al Koufra to the Green Mountain, he was met by Sidi Ahmed Alessawi, the Sheik of Zawyat, Benghazi, and by the tribal leaders of the mountain along with a great number of men from the tribe of Al-Menefa that Sidi Omar belonged to.

"The news I have for you, Sidi Omar, brings no joy to the heart, I'm afraid. Benghazi has been taken by the Italians," Sidi Ahmed informed Sidi Omar in a sorrowful tone.

"This is truly devastating news. We will fight them to the last drop of our blood. This is only a battle, but the war hasn't started yet. They will never have it easy, Ahmed," Sidi Omar replied.

"How are people coping?" one tribal leader asked.

"They are spending their days counting the dead. They are living in a state of fear. They have lost so many of their children. We fought, but we were no match for their heavily armed and well organised army. We lost a lot of men," Sidi Ahmed added. "Please, Lord, give us strength."

"Amen," said all the men.

"Give me a detailed account of what exactly happened from the moment they landed," Sidi Omar asked.

"Well, after the envoy's boat returned to the fleet, we read the letter and it was an ultimatum that the city should surrender, and it gave us 24 hours to consider it. Otherwise the ships would open fire and take Benghazi by force," Sidi Ahmed explained.

"What happened then?"

"It was a huge fleet for such a small city like Benghazi to deal with. But we had made up our minds and decided to fight and resist the invasion. The national and the Turkish officers had managed in those few days to train as many as they could, guns given to those who could use them. The trenches began a few days earlier and foxholes were set everywhere around the city. It was a very tense night and the Italians switched on the spotlights from time to time. I guess they were looking for a white flag as a sign of surrender."

"It must have been very hard for everyone in the city," another tribal leader commented

"Continue, please," Sidi Omar asked politely.

"The next morning we waited anxiously as it became clear that the Italians would open fire at any minute. A few hours later the city was at the mercy of the Italian gunships. It was horrific as the people never saw or heard anything like this before. There was screaming, weeping and crying coming from everywhere as the houses started collapsing over the women and children. Women carried children and their toddlers in their bosoms and holding the youngsters by their hands, they ran away from the city. They randomly shelled Benghazi; no one was safe. We thought the Italians would land their troops in Althama Beach so we moved all our men there. That was a mistake because they moved to the other side of the city."

"So where did they land?" Sidi Omar enquired.

"The seaborne landing invasion began at Jillyana Beach. When the news came, we swiftly moved there. The initial landing had just started so we engaged them immediately and we were able to push them back to the sea."

"Allah Akbar!" one man proclaimed.

"Allah Akbar, Allah Akbar," more men said simultaneously.

"We captured lots of heavy guns and they suffered some casualties. Soon the orders were given to the gunship to start the bombardment in our direction, so we retreated back toward the city." Sidi Ahmed paused for a few seconds before continuing. "The news reached the rural villages, and volunteers were gathering in numbers and they formed a small army under the command of Almasri Basha. We fought bravely in every corner of the city and in Alberka. Sidi Hussein, Alkeesh, and Sidi Abduljelel suffered a lot of casualties."

"They're fighting for something that doesn't belong to them; we're fighting for something worth dying for, and that's the difference between us and them, gentlemen," Sid Omar pointed out.

"Yes, indeed, we were fighting for something more precious to us than to them. It's our home, our women, our children and above all, our dignity," Sidi Ahmed added. "But General Amilio – the commander of the Italian Fourth Army – knew that his troops were no match for our men and fear started infiltrating his men's hearts so he ordered the fleet commander, General Oberi, to begin an assault on the city. Tragedy struck and when we saw the devastating impact on civilians, we had no choice but to give the order to the mayor to form a delegate to discuss the surrender of the city and we retreated to the hills of Benina to join Almasri Basha's camp."

"The men have really done well and it was a wise decision to surrender to save the women and children and what was left for them," a tribal man said.

That night, a negotiating party comprising of the mayor, the Catholic priest and officers of Turkish and national forces, went to the highest building in the city with lanterns and a white cloth. They stood there waving their lanterns and the white cloth as a sign of surrender. It took the fleet some time to spot them. Eventually the bombardment ceased.

Benghazi was burning and smoke rose high from every corner of the city. The heart–wrenching sounds of children wailing, and mothers mourning the loss of their children, continued throughout the night. Fathers called their names in a desperate attempt to locate their sons or daughters and hoped that they were still alive. The devastating aftermath was too big for a peaceful and primitive city to handle.

On the morning of 20 October 1911, Captain Bianco led the troops into the city of Benghazi and raised the Italian flag on top of the government building. They immediately set up checkpoints and soldiers called to the locals' houses, ordering them to give up any weapons they had. The Italians built gallows in every corner of the city and swinging bodies became a common sight. Men were sent to their deaths for the littlest thing, but the Italians called these insignificant acts as "crimes against Italy".

The next few years were no different as the people of Cyrenaica, and the city of Benghazi in particular, called them the "Years of Suffering". In 1912 the Turks signed a peace treaty with the Italians known as the Lausanne Treaty, in which the Turkish surrendered Libya to Italy and started withdrawing their army from Libyan soil, which left Libyans feeling betrayed. The Italians thought this treaty would give them Libya on a golden plate and the Libyans would submit to the order of the Turkish Sultan, but they thought wrong, as the fight was not really with the Ottomans but with the men and women of Libya.

In 1913 the "Black Death" plague struck the city of Benghazi and spread to the Green Mountains, killing a vast number of Libyans. Rats that arrived with the Italian ships were carriers of this disease. Of course, the Italians did everything they could to stop the spread of the plague, but it was too little too late.

1914 was no better, with the arrival of the ruthless African mercenaries coming from Eretria in their thousands to the city of Benghazi to do the dirty work for the Italians as World War I loomed. A year later, Italy took part in the war against Turkey, Austria and Germany, and because of that they needed to deploy troops from Libya to Europe. Knowing that their army would be smaller in Libya, they engaged in peace talks with the Mujahedeen in order to give them time and space to manoeuvre. The attack on the Italian ships by the German submarines meant very little food was reaching the port of Benghazi, as the Italians needed to feed their soldiers first and then their African mercenaries. There was not enough food for the people of the city and the locals seen eating anything. At one time, the seaweed was the daily diet for people and animals too. During those years, the Italians were sending thousands of local men from all over Libya – as punishment for crimes against Italy – to hard labour prisons (which offered dire conditions) across Italy, and the prisoners suffered brutal treatment. Some of them had returned home but for many the fate they received is still unknown. To this day, the Libyans call them "the lost souls of Libyans in the Italian soil".

Once again the people of Barka came face to face with a catastrophic disease. The Black Death struck again in 1917 and this year was known as the "Year of War and Plague". Italy returned from the war victorious in 1918, but its army and country were in a weakened state. Its economy was in a total mess. This led to political unrest across Italy and the rise of organisations, parties and movements. A year later a young man named Benito Mussolini was leading a movement known in Milan as the *camicie nere*, or "the Black Shirts" as they were infamously known and it was the foundation of the Fascist party.

Before the war ended, the Germans and Turks had managed to smuggle Sidi Ahmed Al Shareef from Libya to Turkey for his safety and to use him as a political figure and a thorn in the

Italian's side when needed. Sidi Ahmed appointed Sidi Drees as his successor to lead the Alsanoussian Movement, but Sidi Ahmed never saw Libya again as he died in Mecca in 1933 after he was forced to leave Turkey for political reasons.

For the Libyans and people of Barka, those years of suffering proved that they were nothing compared to the torment that Mussolini and his generals would inflict upon them in the coming years.

Sidi Drees reinforced Sidi Omar Al-Mukhtar and asked him to engage in political talks with the Italians to bring some stability to the region. Sidi Omar was always available whenever the Italians needed to talk and was at the helm of the negotiating table whenever he was asked, but never once to sell his country for personal gain. Sidi Omar was truly a man of integrity, honour and fidelity.

CHAPTER FIVE

The year 1922 was an important year for the Italians and for Libyans. So many things happened that year changed the face of Italy and its policy in Libya. Benito Mussolini and his *camicie nere*, now marched on Rome with hundreds of thousands of supporters, and in his mind was one thing, it was power, and nothing would stop him achieving that. On the other hand, King Victor Emmanuel III knew that any attempt to crush Mussolini would result in disaster as the royal family learned a great deal from the Russian experience and what cruel fate the Tsar and his family had faced. The king appointed Mussolini as prime minster and asked him to form a government and to add to that, he called him the "ll Duce" – the absolute leader. Mussolini formed the Fascist Party, which derived from the Latin word "fasces", which means a bundle of rods wrapped around an axe. Benito Mussolini cancelled all treaties with Libya in 1922 and appointed Marshall Pietro Badoglio as the Governor and the Military Commander of Cyrenaica and Tripolitania, and he ordered what became known as "the Punitive Pacification".

That year Sidi Omar Al-Mukhtar had achieved the final organisation of "Aladwar" – the camps in which every tribe would provide him with a certain amount of men depending on their number, and this figure remained intact throughout the struggle. It meant that if someone lost his life on the battlefield, someone else was ready to fill in, and Sidi Omar appointed a leader in each camp. Tribes would also supply him with provisions for his men, and part of their income in order to buy arms and ammunitions from the bordering countries. Also in that year, the Grand Sonussi, Sidi Drees, fled the country to Cairo, as his life became under threat from the new regime in Italy. He sought international publicity for the Libyan cause and he form allies with the British. Before that, he appointed Sidi Omar as the political negotiator and the military commander of the resistance.

Salem, my father's story as he told it to me.

1922. My father named me Salem after his own grandfather. I was born into a Bedouin family from the Green Mountain. My father's name was Hassan. He was a tall man with a strong build I have the greatest memory of him. He used to take me everywhere with him, even sometimes when he went with the local men with their hunting dogs fetching for porcupines. This was his favourite weekend pastime. Our tribe, like most of the Green Mountain tribes, was nomadic. We followed the rain in the wintertime, sowed the land with wheat or barley, and then moved back to the valleys. Before we headed back to the fields of wheat in the beginning of the summer, to harvest the small piece of land that my Dad owned for the harvest season, all the tribal men and women helped each other. We used to spend weeks, hand and sickles were the only method used. Every time the men covered a big area, then they let the animals move in and feed on the hay. The women catered for the men and went around with water and tea. This was a fun time for us as kids when the wheat stacks made into stack bundles so we could play hide and seek. Then came the part that everyone could join in. It was the time when the grains separated from the stacks, when the bundles put on a huge piece of cloth and then the stacks hammered with sticks. I assisted in any way I could.

After all the grains were stacked in bags, the donkeys would then move it to the village, where some of the grain w used for consumption and the rest for trade. There we spent most of the summer, looking after our small piece of land where figs, grapes grew naturally. Our village overlooked the Green Mountain's big valley where the houses built from wood and stones. My mother's name was Kalthoum. She was in her late 30s and was beautiful in every way as a woman, mother and wife. Mother looked after all of us and she always worked around the clock. Then my grandfather, Muftah, moved in with us at my father's request after my grandmother passed away. I do not really have any memories to recall with her, as I was so young when she departed from this world. My sister, Aisha, was 12 years of age the day we marched to Al-Agaila and I was eight. My father always called her "my crown". Then there was my uncle, Saleh. He was my mother's only brother. He was so great to have around, but he also disappeared for months before we saw him again and so too did my father, and when he came back, he always lost weight. His hair and his white beard got so thick and long. Mother used to say to us that he went to the desert to do business there, but later I learned that my father and uncle were volunteers in Sidi Omar's army. I must say that I missed him a lot when he was not around, but when I got older I was proud of him. He taught me how to love my country, and through him I learned the meaning of belonging.

It had been almost six months when he left us the last time. One day, just before sunset, as my mother was baking the bread in Al-Tannour in the backyard which overlooked the valley, my grandfather was busy cleaning the lanterns and filled them with kerosene. Aisha was in charge of the dinner, which was cooking slowly on a wooden fire and I played with my dog.

"Sidi Muftah, someone is coming over," my mother shouted to my grandfather. My grandfather abandoned what he was doing and moved toward the edge of the valley and put his hand over his eyebrows.

"It's Hassan, my son Hassan!" grandfather cried. We all stood there for a second.

"It's my Dad, it's my father!" I shouted with excitement. He was leading his horse by the reins. Aisha and I ran down to him. My dog, Saiyad, was barking as he zoomed between us, wagging his tail. As soon as he saw us, father dropped the reins and ran toward us, and when we got to him, he knelt down and held Aisha and me in a tight embrace. I felt so safe that I wanted to stay there forever.

"How are you, Dad? We missed you. Where have you been?" I asked with tears in my eyes.

My father was still hugging and kissing us. "I am here, my son. How are you?"

"We're fine, Dad. The village isn't the same without you," Aisha answered.

"Come here, my crown. You really know how to charm a man," my father said with a big grin on his face. At that time my mother and grandfather appeared.

"Mrhaba, Hassan, my son. Come to me," and grandfather hugged him and my father was taking his hand and kissing it. I could see tears in my granddad's eyes. Father was his only child. Then my father turned to Mum and took her in his arms, kissing her forehead.

"Mrhaba, Hassan. How are you?" Mum asked. "We all missed you."

"I'm a bit tired, but in good health and good form," father assured her.

"Let's climb back to the house. Let's not make too much fuss. It might attract the attention of the wrong people, if you know what I mean, my son," my grandfather advised before he turned to lead the way.

Dad held our hands while he was staring at mother with eyes full of love. All this was happening while Saiyad cried and wagged his tail, heralding my father's homecoming. Eventually he got the response he needed from my father.

As soon as we got back to the house, Mum lit another fire and put on a huge pot of water for my father to wash himself. Every time he came back, his hair was longer and curlier, and he looked thinner. His clothes were dirty and were sometimes tattered.

Grandfather removed the saddle and reins from the horse and prepared drink and food for him. The sun disappeared behind the hills and the chirping of crickets begins as darkness fell. My father put on his long, white Jalabiya after washing himself and came to the room where granddad and I sat waiting for him. Mum and Aisha were serving the dinner, which was Dshisha with dry meat and freshly made Tannour bread and In addition, Buttermilk to wash it down. It was a real treat for a Bedouin family. The five of us gathered around the big dish and waited for granddad to start first, as it was tradition and

35

a mark of respect that the eldest always takes the first taste of food before anyone else.

"Besm Allah," said my grandfather while taking a handful of the food and throwing it back into his mouth. "May the Lord bless your hands, Kalthoum. Your food is always tasty," my grandfather said while taking another bite.

"Thank you, Sidi Muftah," Mum replied while she was pushing some dry meat in front of my father's side of the dish. We all noticed that. Aisha and I looked at each other and smiled.

"How is Sidi Omar,?" my grandfather enquired.

"Al hamdulilah, thanks be to God, he's in good form and he keep us going," Dad replied.

"There are so many African mercenaries being deployed to this region and there is a lot of movement by the Italians. There's definitely something going on," my grandfather remarked.

"You just have to be vigilant and alert, Dad," Father told him. Aisha and I did not understand much of the conversation, which continued during dinner. Sometimes I thought they were speaking in different language. Then the conversation focused on us. Aisha and I took advantage of that and started bombarding our father with all sort of questions. Mum and Aisha began cleaning and preparing the little coal stove for a cup of tea and they dished up some dry summer fruits. Then my grandfather lit up a cigarette and the conversation became centred on how the villagers were coping.

"When do you have to go back?" grandfather enquired. This is the question we all wanted to ask.

"By dawn, I'm afraid," my father answered without any hesitation.

"No, Dad, don't go. Please stay a little longer," I begged while crying.

"I wish I could, my son, but I must go. You're very young to understand, but when you are a little older, you'll forgive me for not being with you."

After tea my grandfather stood, grabbed a lamp and pulled his cloak behind him. "Goodnight. I' ll see you before dawn. Inshallah."

"God bless you, Dad. See you at dawn for the prayer," Dad replied. My mother and Aisha were cleaning up. I took my lamp and kissed Dad's hand before I asked him to wake me up for the prayer.

"Well, my son, God bless you. I'll wake you up, but remember you are the man of the house. I need you to be strong." These words made me feel older than I was; they made me more patient and resilient. I made my way to the room that I shared with my sister, Aisha. While our village was sinking into total darkness, our eyes were getting heavier and could not resist the power of sleep.

That night I dreamt I was riding on the horse with my father. I held onto him so tightly while the horse galloped through the valleys of the Green Mountain. Sometimes I felt that Dalam, the horse, was flying through the air. Then we reached the sea. Father held the reins with one hand and pointed to the sea with the other and said,

"Do you know, Salem, that there are other worlds beyond these great waters. I always dreamt that one day I'd ride this big sea, but I think I will not be able to do that but you will, my son, but first you must respect the sea, you have to know that it is so powerful. You have to be ready. You must be well equipped and must arm yourself with the greatest weapon and that is wisdom, otherwise you will drown before reaching the safe shores of the other side. My son, the sea is so big and so profound; in it lies good and evil. It gives but also takes. There is beauty and ugliness contained within. It gives life but it also has the shadows of death dancing not too far away. So remember, that you will lose things that you love, but you will also gain certain things as well. you must arm yourself before you ride the big sea. Do you hear me, Salem?"

My father's a hand shaking me softly and his voice now disturbed my dream. "Salem, wake up, son." I opened my eyes and the sound of waves crashing against the rocks was still in my ears. My father seemed like a giant angel in his long, bright white Jalabiya. "Good morning, Salem, it's dawn. Come pray with us," father said while the aroma of tea with fresh mint from the teapot on the coal stove, drifted into the air.

We prayed together and had tea with Tannour bread. My mother was preparing some provisions for my Dad to take with him. It was dry meat, bread and dry figs. My father and grandfather had just finished saddling the horse.

It was the winter of 1929. I remember that morning well as the four of us stood like soldiers to say goodbye to the leader.

"Look after them, Dad, and look after yourself," my father instructed while he embraced his father. They hugged for what seemed like a lifetime. It was the first time that I saw tears in grandfather's eyes twice in one day.

"You look after yourself, son. Give my regards to Sidi Omar and all the men," my grandfather said while he was trying to conceal his emotions. Grandfather hugged him as if it were the last time he would ever see him. Then Dad turned his attention to my mother and he took a silver chain from around his neck and leaned gently over her shoulder, whispering something in her ears.

My father put his two hands on her shoulders and said, "Take good care of the kids, Kalthoum. They are everything to us. We live for them. You have to be strong. Teach them how to be patient and that in this life there are things that are worth dying for." Dad took my mother into his arms and then he looked at her, wiped the tears from her eyes and kissed her.

"Marbouha. Good luck, Hassan. May the Lord protect you. I'll watch over the children. You go and never worry about them," Mum said trying to comfort him, but she was not successful in holding her tears back. Then my father got down on his knees and held Aisha's hands. Aisha looked so calm and pretty.

"A good daughter is a crown on her father's head and you are my crown. You take good care of your mum and my father. I want you to look after Salem too." Then he hugged her.

"You go, Daddy, and don't worry, we'll look after each other. I can't wait to see you again," Aisha replied with a soft confident voice. Then came the moment that I always dreaded and hated, the moment that I had to say goodbye to my father.

"Come to me, Salem. Come, my son. You're the man of the house now. I'm counting on you. I promise you when I come back I'll take you with me wherever I go." My father took me under his wings. That was how I saw his arms. My father was a giant angel. I cried but never said a word.

Grandfather brought the horse to Dad. He took the reins from my grandfather's hand and, putting his foot on the stirrup, he jumped up on the saddle. In that moment I quickly recalled every little memory we had together. It was a weird feeling that we all shared, knowing that he would never come back to us again. He looked at us for the last time and then Mum hit the horse's rear with her hand to make him move. The horse was making his way down to the bottom of the valley. Dad never looked back and none of us could stop crying.

After a little while my father and Dalam disappeared. It was the last time we saw my father. The crickets stopped and the chanticleers of the village started declaring the birth of a new day.

CHAPTER SIX

General Graziani was sitting behind his desk in his office at his military base in Africa studying some files as part of his daily routine contemplating how and when the time will arrive that he would govern Libya one day?. The ruthless general had built up his reputation through torturing and killing defenceless and vulnerable people, deservedly earning him the name, "The Butcher of Fezzan". Only the knocking on his office door disturbed him from his daydreaming.

"Enter," said the general then door opened and a young officer entered. He saluted the general and stood there waiting for Graziani's reaction.

"What is the problem?" The general asked while his eyes focused on the files.

"A letter from Rome," the young officer replied while nodding in confirmation. The general's eyes were wide with excitement.

"*Consegnarlo a me*," Graziani ordered with his hand out for the letter. The young officer marched closer to the desk and handed the general the letter. Graziani thanked the officer before dismissing him.

When he was alone, Graziani opened the envelope cautiously and then pulled out a small letter and commenced reading it, the frown gradually transformed into a large, beaming smile. Upon finishing the letter, which had come directly from the Fascist Party signed by Mussolini, Graziani crumpled it up and shouted that finally the ll Duce recognised the true men of Italy. The general promoted to Vice Governor of Libya and the Military Governor of Cyrenaica. His dream had come true.

"Finally I can bring more glory to Rome, to ll Duce and the King," the general muttered. Then he made his way to a small drink cabinet he took a bottle of Scotch and a glass and fixed himself a drink. He toasted to a big poster of Mussolini, which hung on the wall behind Graziani's desk.

"To ll Duce," he shouted before throwing the drink down the back of his throat. "Now I can crush those Bedouins, pacify Cyrenaica and root out those rebels at any cost."

It was only three weeks before Graziani received another letter. This time the ll Duce wanted his general to come to Rome. He wanted to show his general that he was preparing him for a bigger glory, but the ll Duce knew little about him and that the general's dreams were bigger and darker than anyone had imagined. Time exposed his true nature, however, later during the Second World War when he came face to face with a formidable and organised army on the Libyan front when almost 200,000 of his troops surrendered to the allies in only a few days. The Fascist Party wanted his head for the disaster and the embarrassment he caused, but Mussolini's intervention saved him. He would have died as a coward.

Graziani wasted no time in preparing for the trip and resigned his previous post to his deputy. A few days later the general's airplane was flying over the Libyan Sahara Desert and he remembered the days where he served as a young officer during the First World War and his time in Tripolitania Italia.

"I can't wait to get to Cyrenaica," the general mumbled to himself while dreaming of how he was going to get Omar Al-Mukhtar and make an example of him, and how he was going to crush the Bedouins along with pacifying the Green Mountain and Cyrenaica.

The general's plane landed on one of Rome's military airbases, but the general was astounded when he saw the reception that Il Duce had prepared for him. He was received like a Roman commander who just returned victorious from a long and bloody battle on the Empire's frontiers and the emperor was there himself to receive him and hail him as a hero. Graziani was very popular in Italy, especially among young Italians who thought of him as, "the general that could never be defeated". Graziani was taken straight to the Italian parliament where he gave a speech glorifying Italy, the King and Il Duce.

That night Graziani dined with Mussolini and his Generals, sipping alcohol and exchanging compliments while the musical orchestra played gentle symphonies in the background.

Suddenly the music stopped and the order given to the guests for total silence. The Il Duce was about to give his own speech. He stood and put his hands on his hips and gazed with extreme assuredness at everyone.

"Signores, e Signori, you're all welcome," he shouted. "Tonight we celebrate the arrival of our great general and good friend." He raised a glass of wine and said, "From this day onwards, the general shall be addressed as 'The Pacifier of Libya and the Pacifier of Cyrenaica'."

They celebrated well into the night, but before Mussolini excused himself, he leaned on his general's shoulder and whispered that he wanted to see him in his office the next day at noon. The general continued for a while, revelling in the attention he received from the men and women. When he slept later, he dreamt about being the Il Duce.

As ordered, he was at Mussolini's office at noon. A black car carrying the general arrived outside the Fascist Party's headquarters. A young officer opened the door for Graziani and stood firm while saluting him. The general climbed the marble steps gracefully and at the top he turned right to enter a long corridor. There were soldiers lining each side all the way to the end. They saluted the general as he passed them. At the end of the corridor, there was a big door where two armed fascist special guards stood at each side of it. Once the general stood outside the door, the two guards saluted him. Graziani fixed the jacket of his uniform and with his two hands, pulled down his cap. Together, the guards opened the door by pulling a handle on either side of it. Once the general was inside, they closed the door.

Benito Mussolini stood by the huge glass window, which overlooked the headquarters' square. His back was to the general and his arms on his hips. Mussolini's baldhead shone as the spring sun hung in the middle of the sky. When Mussolini faced the general, Graziani saluted him with the Fascist party

Roman-Nazi salute. Mussolini saluted him in return and then the general greeted him.

"*Buongiorno*, Il Duce."

"*Buongiorno, il mio amigo*," Mussolini replied while he walked toward him with his hand up in the air. "I hope you enjoyed yourself last night."

"*Si*, I did, sir, and I was honoured to be in your presence."

"We shall celebrate this occasion with a toast," Mussolini said, beckoning to follow him to a cabinet and celebrate his friend's promotion. He took out two crystal glasses and a bottle of whiskey. Then he poured two good measures into the glasses and handed one to Graziani.

"*Molte grazie, Signore*," Graziani said with gratitude while reaching for the glass.

"*Sguardo, Generale*," Mussolini told Graziani to look at the huge, colourful map of the world, which was painted on the office wall. "Look, General, the English have succeeded in controlling all these parts of the world and look where the French have gone. I have sent so many governors to Libya but they all failed, in my opinion. I can't afford to lose any more soldiers. We are under pressure from the media and the families of those soldiers who come back in coffins, and that's why I chose you, General. You are the one who can pacify Cyrenaica."

Graziani bowed and thanked Mussolini for the trust he placed in him and vowed not to let him down. "I will demolish the Bedouins, but I need you to give me some guarantees and secure permission from the Fascist Party that I'll be given the green light to have total freedom to execute my plan."

Mussolini smiled as he answered, "I'm pleased that someone finally has a plan."

Mussolini drank to that and toasted to Graziani's good health. They both threw back their drinks and grimaced as it hit their throats.

Then Graziani boldly added, "In order to do that, I will not have any consideration for the Italian nor the International laws. Also I will not accept my appointment unless I get the go– ahead, Il Duce, but I can guarantee you that I'll bring the

Green Mountain revolt into total submission and crush Omar Al-Mukhtar's skull."

Mussolini promised to grant everything the general asked for and said, "Go now and waste no time. We need Libya. It's our gateway to Africa, General."

Graziani put his glass on the table and fixed his cap before saluting the Il Duce and departed from the room. Just as he was about to leave, Mussolini called him back and Graziani froze without facing him.

Mussolini ordered that the Bedouins were to be crushed and for Omar Al-Mukhtar, "*Rompere il collo*", he wanted that man's neck broken. The general smiled and marched toward the door.

The next day, Graziani, now with the title of "The Pacifier of Libya and the Pacifier of Cyrenaica", flew to Cyrenaica and landed in Benghazi, where similar celebrations were held for his appointment. A couple of days after that, Graziani was busy putting his plan together along with Signore Emillio Debono, the Chairman of the Italian colonies, and Signore Marshal Pietro Badoglio, the General Governor of Libya, and sent the dossier to Rome for endorsement by the Fascist Party and its leader, Il Duce Benito Mussolini

CHAPTER SEVEN

As the general was waiting anxiously for the go–ahead from Rome to execute his plan, Sidi Omar Al-Mukhtar gave Graziani something to think about in the meantime. The first week of the general's new appointment was not something worth celebrating. Sidi Omar and his men, on 11 April 1930, launched a surprise attack on an Italian unit in the region of Al-Faydia, The Italian unit was completely destroyed.

* * *

When Graziani received the news, he was in his office among top rank army officials from all divisions. The general hid the embarrassment.

Graziani said that it was rather bad news and added, "Gentlemen, there is nothing to fear. I have a plan, and once I get the go–ahead, I will crush those Bedouins and their leader."

Graziani did not sleep that night and later wrote in his memoirs that the battle of Al-Faydia was a great loss for the Italians and that Omar Al-Mukhtar was "a natural fighter who truly loved his country and defended his religion vigorously".

In the morning, the general paced up and down the floor of his office anxiously. A few hours later, the phone rang and the general grabbed the receiver in a frantic motion.

"*Pronto*," said the general. "Yes, it's Graziani speaking."

It was Marshall Badoglio.

The general put down the phone and sighed with relief. "Finally, now I will earn the name 'the Pacifier of Cyrenaica'!" The General immediately called for an emergency meeting with his top ranking officers from all divisions. No one would stand in his way now.

Graziani, in full military uniform, was in his office at the headquarters in the city of Benghazi, standing in front of a huge map of Libya.

He addressed the officers by saying that Omar Al-Mukhtar's days were numbered and he would proceed with his plans without any further delay. "I want you to listen very carefully and execute my orders without any consideration for any law. There's no more time for treaties, truces and delegations with the rebels. We'll destroy Omar and his men once and for all!"

General Graziani was feared and well respected among his army. He pointed with his stick to the Libyan–Egyptian border. "We will build a fence of barbwire along the Libyan–Egyptian border 300 kilometres long, a metre and a half in height and three metres in width," the general explained before was politely interrupted by one of his officers.

"*Scusa,* Signore, what are the objectives?"

"Well, Signori Colonnello Fornari, the objectives are firstly, to deny Omar Al-Mukhtar any economic supply and arms smuggled in from Egypt and secondly to prevent them from retreating and regrouping and this, gentlemen, is my first plan. My second plan is to deprive the people of Barka their homes. We will take them to the worst and harshest lands in the Libyan Sahara. They will burn during the day and freeze by night. We will confiscate their lands, burn their fields, block their wells, and we will use their animals for our consumption and the rest will go to the Motherland. We'll put the people in concentration camp, feed them very little and they will never quench their thirst. Gentlemen, we will even deprive them the air that they breathe."

The general looked deep into the eyes of all his officers. "Before anyone asks me, I'll tell you the reason for that. First, we will deny them their mountain stronghold. Then we will cut any supply of food and money to Al-Mukhtar and his men, finally preventing any more men joining him. There is more, gentlemen. There are hard days ahead of you and you must listen. I will not accept any excuses. I want results and at any cost, so you must follow everything I say."

Each of the officers eyed one another, but kept their concerns and reservations to themselves.

Graziani inhaled a large breath, pointed to the middle of the map with his stick and continued, "Finally, gentlemen, we will take Al Koufra–"

An officer interrupted the general by putting up his hand.

"*Si*, Signori," the general said.

"*Scusa*, Signore, why Al Koufra?" the officer asked before highlighting a few valid points. "It's deep in the Libyan Sahara Desert, hard to reach and surely would be a great risk to our men."

"Bravo, Capitano Bini. You may sit." Then the general continued, "The taking of Al Koufra is part of my plan and yes, Capitano." The general directed his eyes toward Captain Bini, "It will be hard and harsh on our army, but if we capture this territory, we would then suffocate Omar Al-Mukhtar and bring those Sonussis to their knees, now you see, Al Koufra must be taken. First we will deny the rebels their stronghold in the desert and then we will cut the supply of men to Al-Mukhtar. When all this is done, then we will receive a great honour from our people and the King."

The general then threw his stick on the desk and continued, "Gentlemen, you have heard and now you must deliver. You may go now and prepare yourselves for many weeks of hard work. You will be informed of all the details shortly."

The officers stood and saluted their general before making their way to the door. When the last officer left, Graziani pulled a drawer and took out Omar Al-Mukhtar's spectacles, "Today I crush your glasses, tomorrow your neck." The general said.

Work was going as planned and at a rapid speed since Grazini oversaw it himself. He brought a labour force of thousands of Italians, Africans and even Libyan men and he gave orders that work will be around the clock.

"Signori, Brachi," the general shouted.

"*Si*, Signore Graziani," the colonel replied.

"I want you to organise checkpoints and patrolling units along the fence," the general commanded while getting into his military car.

Within weeks, the general was deep in the Libyan Sahara, and he was standing on a sandy hill on the outskirts of the desert city. He was looking through his binoculars. "Gentlemen, this is Al Koufra. Go and take it with or without its people. Show no mercy and take no prisoners," Graziani said while handing the binoculars to one of his officers.

Al Koufra looked so peaceful and quiet, palm trees surrounded it, and they stood like giants protecting the city. To avoid any embarrassment, Graziani prepared a very strong army consisting of 25 military airplanes, 700 Italian officers and 3,000 African mercenaries, and hundreds of guns and armoured vehicles. All this against a small desert city of 200 fighters.

The general gave the orders for the air force to start their raids on the city. The Italians used poisonous gases against the people of Al Koufra.

After a few hours of devastating the city, Italian troops began their ground assault. The Bedouin people of Al Koufra weren't prepared for anything like this. They did not know what hit their city as it was the first time ever for those hopeless people to see airplanes. The destruction was massive. No one escaped the atrocity. Two hundred fighters halted Graziani for two days before he entered the city to see what he had inflicted upon the peaceful people of Al Koufra. . Graziani did not stop at that, but ordered the air force to follow those civilians who escaped toward the open Sahara and to burn them. For seven days, the airplanes flew and scoured the ground, shooting at anything that moved.

"This is Al Koufra. It's yours now. Do whatever you want with it," the general told his troops while standing posing for the camera. The news reached Italy and the media hailed Graziani as "the general that cannot be defeated".

The troops took the general's words very literally and began their brutal acts of terror against the women and children of the city. The raping and destruction continued for many days. The attack on Al Koufra was a crime against humanity, showing the true face of fascism. Graziani did not want to take Al Koufra, but he was utilising systematic and callous tactics of ethnic–cleansing against the Libyans.

Days later, when the smoke had cleared, the ugly picture of the attack started to become apparent. Hundreds of families had died in their homes. The streets were full of dead bodies; children and even babies did not escape the horrendous crimes. The sound of women wailing were all could heard in that city for years to come.

The capture of the small city of Al Koufra had a devastating impact on the people of Benghazi, the Green Mountain and Sidi Omar. Worse was yet to come as the years of misery still lay ahead with the completion of Graziani's sinister plan and the misery would come in the form of concentration camps. More than 100,000 people forced against their will to leave their homes and march into the concentration camps. While there, they were subjected to the most barbaric and gruesome treatment. Tents of concentration camps were set up in the harshest conditions like Sloug, Al-magroon and Al-brega. These names will be engrave in the Libyan peoples' memories for many generations to come. But the concentration camp of Al-agaila would be remembered most for the inhumane treatment that the people there faced. It was Graziani's orders to degrade those Bedouins to a level never before witnessed by humans. They endured systematic starvation, deprivation of medical help, forced labour, rape and the humiliation of not being able to answer nature's call in private as toilets were out in the open. It was hard for a society that prided itself on its decency and privacy.

The Al-agaila concentration camp is a shameful reminder of Graziani's service to the Italian people in the Mussolini era. Sixty five thousand people perished in these camps. They were set in wastelands, tents behind barbwires, guarded by armed Italians and ruthless African mercenaries. Half of the people of Cyrenaica's population were marched to these camps under the heat of the sun during the day on hard roads not really fit for walking on, and in the freezing desert weather by night. Some of them had to walk 1,000 kilometres. Others were lucky and marched the distances of 600 kilometres. Graziani was adamant that they reached those places in the time he chose. By his orders, if anyone lagged behind to be shot dead.

His orders executed and hundreds died of thirst before reaching the camps of sorrow and death. Graziani had succeeded; these sadistic acts did suffocate Al-Mukhtar and his men. Supplies of men and arms from the Green Mountain soon ceased. Weapons smuggled in from Egypt and volunteers from the desert dried up. Sidi Omar and his men forced to eat leaves off the trees and drink the rain that fell. Sidi Omar and his men, however, valiantly fought the Italians for another year.

* * *

Our march to the hill began one afternoon in the summer of 1930 after a beautiful, quiet, sunny day. I was playing with Saiyad not far away from the house, as my mother and Aisha were preparing lunch on a wooden fire in the backyard, waiting for the return of my grandfather from his daily work on our land at the top of the mountain. Suddenly something caught my mother's attention as she stood up placing her hand in front of her forehead she shielded her eyes from the sun. There were hundreds of Italian and African soldiers making their way down to our village accompanied by military vehicles.

"Salem, Salem, where are you, son?" Mum cried.

"I'm here, Mum, playing with Saiyad," I replied without a care in the world.

"Come over here. I see the Italians coming down. There must be something going on." I detected a trace of fear in her voice.

Aisha stood next to Mum and said, "Maybe they're looking for Sidi Omar's men or searching for arms. Don't worry, mother."

At that moment, my grandfather came running toward us, panting very loudly.

"Kalthoum, let's waste no time. Gather whatever you can take with us. Aisha, give your mother a hand. They're coming to take us. They forced the people of the hills out of their houses," my grandfather said while catching his breath.

Within minutes, the whole village was in utter chaos as the shouting became louder.

"Go inside your houses; the Italians are here!" yelled one old man.

The sound of the soldiers' boots was like thunder as they closed in on the village. My mother gathered whatever she could; some clothes for me and Aisha, some bread, dry meat, and a gallon of water. Grandfather packed a few things for himself while putting his cloak around body. Then the soldiers burst into the house, shouting vulgar profanities at us. They spoke in a very broken Bedouin accent and in Italian.

One soldier pushed my grandfather and shouted. "Come on. Get out, you fucking Bedouins!"

"Mercy, please, he is an old man," my mother cried. My dog was barking at them relentlessly as an African soldier pushed my mother.

"Don't touch my mother!" I roared while pushing him. He did not hesitate in kicking my leg very hard. Saiyad was about to attack them when one soldier hit him with the butt of his rifle. I feared for him so I ordered the dog to leave. Saiyad whimpered and ran outside through the back door. My mother grabbed us by the hands and ran toward the door.

As we got outside, the villagers gathered in large groups. They all looked stunned, and they carried whatever their hands could take. Soldiers aimed their guns at us, while the mercenaries took everything from the houses, piled them outside and set fire to them. The officers gave orders for the march while the African soldiers were stealing whatever they could: money, clothes and even cutleries. They were sordid and heartless men.

As we reached the top of the hill, I looked down at the village; smoke rose from every corner, the dogs were barking and our lunches were still cooking. Some of those people glanced at their beloved village for the last time. The march continued as the hills and valleys began disappearing behind us. Dust rose up from the ground as people and animals marched together.

Graziani's Italian soldiers allowed us to take a small number of sheep, goats and cows only to discover later that this was for their own benefit as food to fill their bellies.

The numbers grew as more people from other regions merged with ours. Sounds of donkeys braying and the bleating of the goats and sheep entwined with the shouting of people looking for their loved ones. It became very difficult to contain each family. The more we walked, the harder each road surface became to walk on and there was not much food on the surrounding land but only thorn plants. My mother held onto us so tightly that the sweat slipped through her fingers, but not once did she let go. Grandfather was behind us to make sure that we did not drift away.

We marched for the entire day without any break. Vehicles made dust clouds behind which made it more difficult for people to walk. Areterian soldiers were lashing people with their whips. Night had already fallen and orders given for people to stop and sit. It was one hard day and the scorching sun had done its damage. People were exhausted, hungry and thirsty. African soldiers started to make fires and number of lambs slaughtered, but it was only for the Italians' and African mercenaries' benefit. My mother opened the swag that she brought from home and gave us a bit of bread and dry meat, and then she gave us a good measure of water.

"There's no time to chat, Salem, Aisha. Try and get as much rest as you can because tomorrow we might have to walk very far again," Mum said.

The Italians and the African mercenaries were enjoying their feast and they never offered anyone anything. No bullets fired that day. My grandfather took his cloak from around his body and we formed a circle, then we put the cloak around us. I put my head on my mother's lap and started thinking about my father. We had not seen him since that dawn. That night I dreamt that Saiyad and I were chasing the birds on the hills and meadows of the Green Mountain.

Dawn crept in but the skies were not fully bright yet, some old men were calling people to perform the dawn prayer. That was the last time we prayed during our march, as orders were given that no more prayers to be performed until we reached the place we were going to. No one knew what fate awaited us.

The march began once again, and by the fourth day, sounds of gunfire heard in the wasteland few times a day. At the sound of each gunshot, men and women were saying in unison, "We are from God, and to God we shall return", but never looked back. My grandfather was now beginning to show some signs of fatigue as he started drifting away from us. Mum turned quickly while holding us and gave him some encouragement.

"Hajj Muftah, we really need you. Come hold my hand, please, those soldiers have no hearts," Mum cried.

"Move, you old Bedouin, or you know what you're going to get. A bullet in your head in case you have forgotten," one soldier barked while poking him with a stick.

"No one dies before his day," grandfather replied. This aggravated the officer and he struck my beloved grandfather twice on the head.

"Leave him alone. He is an old man!" I yelled at the soldier. Mum feared the worst so she grabbed me and hollered at my grandfather,

"Move, Sidi Muftah. Aisha and Salem need you. Please don't give them any excuse; they're ruthless people!"

Mum's words had the desired effect and gave my grandfather something to make him stay with us a little longer. The soldiers were going around and giving people a piece of bread and water twice a day. Sometimes the march stopped for a little while to bury the old and the infants who could not bear these harsh conditions.

On the seventh day, the infamous AlKebli winds were looming. Its winds blew with such speed, carrying with it the grains of red sand, and they are very hot winds that would burn the face off anyone. As they started getting closer, a man appeared with a long white beard. He was tall, seemed strong, and a little younger than my grandfather was.

"It's Alkebli winds. Keep your heads down and hold each other tightly. For all the women with infants and babies, please put them on your backs and cover them with the drapes. Women and men should give their headscarves to the younger boys and girls. Be prepared, it will reach us any minute." He went from one place to another, motivating people and giving them encouragement and help and he held a woman by her hand. I guessed she was his wife. He reminded me of my father.

The winds reached us and we marched through it though it was difficult, as it seemed that some sort of force was pushing us backwards. Then suddenly I heard my mother shouting and it was difficult to see or hear anything.

"Sidi Muftah, where are you?

Salem, can you see your grandfather anywhere?" Mum asked in a loud voice.

"No, Mum, I can't!" I answered. "Granddad, Granddad" I called out in vain for few minutes. Then I heard him calling me. He was at my side.

"Don't worry, Salem, I'm here," he shouted.

"Come closer to us," I yelled back. We moved closer to him but as we reached him, he collapsed. We all knelt down and tried to help him up but all our attempts failed. He was completely exhausted.

"Come closer to me, Salem. I don't think I will make the journey. You must look after your mum and your sister," my granddad said while breathing heavily.

"Come on, we'll help you," I said, trying to encourage him on, but I could see from the weary look in his eyes that our words and efforts were futile.

At that moment an Italian soldier came over to us and started shouting, "Move, you fucking bastard Bedouin", while he kicked him. This time I could not help myself and lunged at him, cursing at him for the first time and it was in Italian, "*Bastardo*" as I guessed that it must be a bad word.

Around that time there were calls coming from everywhere for the marching to stop. The officer laughed and said, "*Sei fortunate, bastardo*," then kicked granddad very hard before disappearing into the crowd.

"We're truly lucky," my mother said while lifting my grandfather.

That night was the worst night since the march began. We all huddled together, shielded by my granddad's cloak. The wailing of the wind was mixed with babies crying, which added to the misery of this march.

By dawn, the wind had quietened and the dust settled, but people burned, their throats were dry and their spirit was broken. The march resumed shortly after a sip of water and a piece of bread handed out. Some people who brought tealeaves were able to make tea but they had to bribe the soldiers. My grandfather's feet were beginning to fail him.

"Kalthoum," he said, "you must listen to me. I beg you to let me stay. I can't walk any longer. Please take the children and go," my grandfather pleaded but his pleas were ignored, as my mother would not abandon her father-in-law.

"We will not let you die by the guns of those horrible people. You must keep walking. Maybe we're almost there," Mum, answered trying to persuade him.

"There's no point. I'll collapse at any minute," granddad replied and then he leaned on our mother's shoulder and whispered something. Tears fell from Mum's eyes as my grandfather handed her his cloak. Soldiers came and kicked him, but my mother did not delay, holding our hands tightly and weeping like a baby. We all cried but kept moving and never looked back. Few minutes elapsed, and then we heard the sound of gunfire engulfing the arid land.

On the tenth day, and after 16 hours of walking each day under the blazing sun of the desert and cold windy nights, we reached Al-agaila – the Camp of Suffering. From the distance, the thousands of tents looked like the heads of devils. This was where I spent a year and where I would learn the meaning of survival. This was where humanity revealed its ugly side, murdering and slaughtering innocent men, women and children. In this hellhole, in the space of 12 months I was transformed into an old man, and I left with physical and psychological wounds. I learned that the wounds do not heal, but we learn how to cope and live with them.

Once we reached the gates of Al-agaila, the Italian and Areterian soldiers were there waiting for us. The Italians armed with guns and the African mercenaries armed with sticks. African soldiers dressed funny; they wore a red fez on their heads, button-less jackets that usually opened and with nothing underneath it. They were barefooted and wore short trousers.

The reception we got from the soldiers was unlike anything I had ever seen before. They were so malevolent and utterly soulless. When we arrived at Al-agaila, the desert sunburnt our faces, our feet swollen, with cuts and bruises, our lips were cut and our throats were very dry. Our hair and clothes covered with red sand from those winds. We were dreaming of water, food and a bed, but that was not what we received. they beat us for no reason and spat at. The vulgarity and obscenities they used were so distasteful that it made women put their fingers in their ears. Our mother was clutching us as if she would never let go. Al-agaila was as if it derived from hell: an arid land, nothing but thorns and sand in the ground and a blazing sun in the sky.

When we arrived at Al-agaila, I was eight years old. Shouting and screaming seemed to be coming from everywhere and the soldiers on top of the watchtowers trained their guns at us no matter where we moved. Soldiers put us in long lines in a big open area. Later, the soldiers were using it for their daily training and for punishment that we received. After they instructed us to form several rows, they ordered us to be silent. Then this man in full military uniform appeared from behind the officers. He seemed to be in charge as everyone was saluting him. A Libyan man who acted as his interpreter followed him. He looked at us for a moment or two with a mean scowl, and he possessed an air of arrogance about him. The mean-looking commander was shouting in Italian, pausing from time to time to give the interpreter a chance to translate.

"Listen, you Arab Bedouins, from this moment onwards this is going to be your home and that's because you helped Omar

Al-Mukhtar by supplying him with men, food, money and arms. You will be here until further orders from his Excellency the Pacifier of Cyrenaica, General Rodolfo Graziani. You must listen very carefully to all the points I'm going to list to you and whoever tries to rebel or even disobey, this will be his or her fate." He pointed to the grim sight of the gallows, which was set not far from where we stood. "Firstly, do not disobey any orders given to any of you, either by the Italians or Areterian soldiers. Secondly, no one allowed near the barbwire. Anyone caught near there, will face this." Again, he pointed to the gallows. "You will be working collecting wood, cooking and cleaning with total obedience. Thirdly, anyone who comes with any form of complaint we will punish him or her, and that goes for everyone including women and children. Consider yourselves lucky because the Italian government has found you a home. Glory to Italy, the King, and Il Duce." The commander finished his speech and then gave orders to the soldiers to escort us to our tents.

The sun had completely disappeared behind the horizon and darkness soon prevailed. A cold chill felt around the camp, as the desert gets cold by night. Before that, they gave us a pillow and two military blankets each: one as a bed and the other as a cover, and a metal bowel to use for food and another for drink.

"Come, Aisha, give me a hand. We have to make our bed. They might come to inspect it," Mum said. The Italians nominated one Libyan to be in charge of over ten tents and they gave them a stick and oil lamp. Some of these men proved to be mean and heartless and soon they used their power by shouting at us loudly. It dinner, and each man led the inhabitants of ten tents in a line. We were holding our metal bowels and were shattered and hungry, and after queuing for a long time, we passed by the African soldiers. They were standing behind large pots and held big ladles in their hands. They told us it was vegetable soup and fresh bread, but the truth, it was only hot water with hardly any vegetables in it and very hard piece of bread. We took it back to the tent and sat on the floor. I was dipping the bread in the soup to soften it. We finished very quickly and Mum took us under her arms. All three of us cuddled as mother prayed while I drifted into a deep sleep.

Dawn broke and another day was born, but the shouting of Italian guards and African mercenaries became louder and louder. Mum, Aisha and I were already up as all Bedouins woke at dawn. Our muscles ached from that terrible march. Soon we were standing in lines. The breakfast was tea with a piece of brown bread, and that continued to be the breakfast for the whole time that I was there. Then some men ordered to follow a group of Italian soldiers to go outside the camp to fetch some wood. Others given orders to clean the camp from all the thorn desert plants. Women assigned to brush outside the tents they handed them brooms made from skinny branches bundled together.

The next day the prisoners of Al-agaila discovered there were no toilet facilities and no running water except for the daily measure that we have to drink. Defecation and urination was the ultimate dilemma for the men and women, especially for a decent, conservative Muslim nation. For us kids it was not much of a problem as we used to hide behind the tents and answer nature's call without much care. I noticed that the men and women were gathering small stones and hid them in their pockets. Later I learned that they used it to clean themselves after defecation.

Women used to go together to form a circle to shield a woman from the men and soldiers while performed a bodily function.

Graziani knew exactly what he meant when he ordered his soldiers to treat us like animals, and that is why he deprived us of running water and decent working toilet facilities, as he knew that water and decency are essential for Muslims for cleaning and for their daily prayers. Not only did they treat us like animals in Al-agaila, but they also forgot that we were humans. The first days were hard and slow and food scarcely handed out. We were starving and malnourished.

The following weeks proved to the men and women of Al-agaila that this place was not going to be home, but instead sheer hell, as their daily work became intolerable. Jobs created to exhaust and demoralise us as collecting faeces from one end of the camp to the other and then bring it back to the same place. This chore carried out from sunrise to sunset and by the end of the day, we would bury it in a big hole.

Bubaker was the first person I have made contact with.

"Hi, how are you? I haven't seen you here before," I said making conversation.

"Yes, that's true. I am from the other side of the camp. I was trying to see if I could spot someone I knew from back home," he replied.

"I live in that tent." I pointed to ours. "I share it with my mother and sister."

"So, where are you from?" he asked.

"Well, we are from the Green Mountain region. You?"

"I am from Albtnan. It's a nice place. I really miss it. What's your name?"

"Salem, Salem Bu–Ayesha. And yours?"

"I am Bubaker. What do you think of those black soldiers? They're weird." Bubaker always squinted or made funny expressions while he spoke.

"Yes indeed. They're funny, especially the way they dress, but they're mean. Do you know that they're mercenaries?"

"What does that mean?"

"Well, it means that they come from different places and work for money, that's what my grandfather said."

"Listen; there are quite a few boys I met here, so maybe we should have a game of something. What do you think?" Bubaker suggested.

"Yes, it sounds good. We'll do something like that soon," I replied. Then Bubaker shook hands with me and ran behind through the tents, vanishing in seconds in order to avoid couple of mercenary soldiers. He was ten years of age and my first friend in the concentration camp.

In the next few days, Bubaker started making regular visits to our side of the camp and each time he had a different friend. Before we knew it, there were five of us. We used to meet very early in the morning to go and watch the Italian soldiers doing their daily training. No one seemed to know how long we were going to be here. Some men said that it was only a matter of time and then they will release us. Others said that our hope of returning to our places all hung on the capture of Sidi Omar. However, the majority thought that this was our new home and the sooner we got used to it, the easier life would become. Later I learned that the men who said this were the most logical and wise because they wanted to prepare people for their long stay here.

My mother called my name many times a day, making sure that I was around and had not gone far from her. Aisha was like my mother's shadow; she followed her everywhere. All of the young girls never left their mothers' or grandmothers' sights. I could never understand this but later I would come face to face with the terrible truth.

My shoes worn-out due to the march. The hot ground and the thorns really had gotten the better of my shoes, but my mother always came up with something to patch them.

Weeks had gone by very slowly. The hot days, cold nights, the unmerciful thirst and scarcity of water took its toll on us. By the end of the first month, unrest began to show, as some men were very angry at the way we treated by the Italians and they asked their Libyan gaffers who were in charge of the tents to take their demands to build toilet facilities at any cost to the Italian officer in charge of the camp. However, they had forgotten that toilets deliberately not provided to degrade us and to strip us of our dignity. The outcome of their demands was very harsh and the punishment was severe, as those men were taken from their tents by force in an inhumane fashion. They were stripped down to their underwear, their hands and feet were tied to small sticks lying flat on the ground. The men were there for three days and three nights, getting nothing but water twice a day, and received many lashes. When they released them, they could not walk but crawled to their tents instead.

Consternation spread amongst us and people felt that this was where they were going to die. When people are desperate and cornered, however, they find themselves fighting for survival.

Now men and women began screaming day and night for help for their babies and small kids, as there was an outbreak of fever in the camp. Their screams for help unfortunately ignored and instead of giving any kind of assistance, those women punished in a barbaric manner by ripping their clothes and punching them until they fell. The sadistic soldiers then lashed the poor women numerous times with their whips. It was hard to see your loved ones wasting away in front of you and not being able to do anything about it.

Shortly after the horrific whipping and beatings, the death cart appeared and Libyan men assigned to the new role of being in charge of it. The death cart went around the camp all day with men walking behind it with pickaxes, spades and shovels. Many times a day the gates opened to let them through to bury the corpses outside the camp.

Our suffering continued, wounds got infected and diseases spread. Crying and mourning the dead became a permanent sound with the ghastly shadow of death always looming over our camp. The first three months were the easiest compared to what about to come.

* * *

I was worried about Bubaker, as I had not seen him in a few weeks. The idea of going to the other side looking for him was constantly on my mind. Only my mother's constant reminder of not to wander outside our row prevented me from doing so. Then one afternoon, Bubaker appeared from nowhere, he was standing before me.

"Here you are, Bubaker. How are you? I was thinking about you. Why didn't you come the last few weeks?" I asked with excitement.

"I'm good, Salem, thank you. My grandfather got very sick and he died. He died in his sleep," Bubaker explained in a sorrowful tone.

"I'm so sorry to hear that," I replied sorrowfully.

"There's more. Two weeks later, my grandmother passed away. My mom told me that our grandmother got an infection in her leg and died. I know you lost your grandfather too." Bubaker put a comforting hand on my shoulder. "How are things with you?"

"I'm fine. Mum and Aisha are good. I'm only worried now about my shoes. Look, you can see my toes," I answered, whilst trying to wiggle my toes. Bubaker laughed and I was glad that I had cheered him up. Then Bubaker moved his hat and lowered his head.

"Look, Salem, one of those horrible soldiers hit me with his stick so hard I nearly fainted. I was trying to help an old man who fainted during his daily work. It was bad. If it wasn't for Sidi Rajab, it would be worse as he shaved all the hair around the wound." Bubaker talked about his wound as if it was nothing. I really looked up to him. He was such a brave child.

"Wow, that's big! Who is Sidi Rajab? I think I heard of that name during the march to here. Was he a big, tall man with a thick black and grey beard?" I asked.

"Yes, that's Sidi Rajab. You described him quite well. Do you know him?"

"No, not really, but I saw him during our march, running around helping people. He looks a bit like my father except he's much older."

"I see, but yes he's a good man and his wife, Amina is a good woman, too. They both help people." Bubaker eyes now switched to something behind me and when I turned around, I saw few soldiers coming toward us. "Assalamu alaikum," he said while grabbing his Jalabiya above his knees with one hand and holding his hat with the other, he ran before vanishing like a ghost.

"Walaikum Assalam," I replied but he was gone. My mother called me and I answered promptly.

At night, families went to their tents to seek rest from the endless suffering when Al-agaila enveloped in total darkness. Then the screaming commenced declaring a death, and the moaning of people nursing their wounds mixed with sick babies crying, became louder. The creaking of the death cart's wheels sent shivers down all our spines. Nine times out of ten, many of the people in Al-agaila were sleepless. Only the sound of the soldiers' boots passing by our tent and their evil laughter made my mother hold Aisha even tighter and her prayers drowned out the harrowing noises that surrounded us.

CHAPTER EIGHT

Eagles circled the sky above the camp. It was noon and Al-agaila was like a place from someone's worst nightmare. Everyone was looking for the shade, even the deadliest serpents and scorpions of the arid land of death sought shelter to cool down, but for the people of the camp, it was business as usual. I was sitting on the steps of the bunkhouse watching a column of ants moving endlessly. I put my finger in front of them and the leader of the ants stopped to feel my finger and then changed direction.

Not far from me was a mercenary sitting by the wall of the bunkhouse, desperately seeking, cool wind to blow across his face to cool him down. He pushed his fez forward to cover his eyes from the strong sunlight. He swatted the irksome flies from his face. A devilish idea popped into my little head and without delay or any hesitation, I found myself gathering small stones and every time he got a moment's peace from the flies, I hit him with one on the head. With a lazy finger, he pushed his fez up to see what was going on around him. The mercenary's eyes were half opened but could see nothing except the flies. I repeated the same action lots of times and the fun part began when he lost his temper and started swearing in his own language, which sounded so funny. When I started giggling, he noticed my presence and looked at me with one eye closed and the second I was ready to throw another one, he jumped up screaming, "It's you, Bastardo, you little Bedouin!"

I ran and he gave chase. I laughed with all my heart as I zigzagged between the tents in order to lose him. but my laughter did not last long because when I got nearer to our section, the Italian soldiers were dragging about five men to be punished. They were tied onto wooden poles and Areterian soldiers began lashing them with their whips. Sidi Rajab was one of them. I was watching from behind a tent. I could see Mum and other women standing watching in despair with tears falling from their eyes. I went straight to our tent. Aisha was there saying a prayer. I did not interrupt her and went straight to where my mother hid a little can of water. She saved some drops of water from her share every day and used it to clean us with it after a little while by dipping cloths into it and clean under our arms and around the neck. It was a very useful technique. I took the can and carefully made my way to the men. I made sure that the soldiers had left after punishing the men severely. It was a scorching hot day and I went to them one by one. I gave each a small sip to wet their dry lips. Then I came face to face with Sidi Rajab, the man who reminded me of my father.

"Please take a sip, Sidi Rajab," I said while looking over my shoulder because I did not want to face the Italian soldiers' wrath.

"May the Lord reward you, boy. You're a very brave child," he said in his deep voice. "But how did you know my name?"

"I saw you during the march. You were helping us."

"Yes, you're the kid who lost his grandfather. What is your name, son?" Sidi Rajab asked with eyes full of admiration for my act of kindness.

"Salem Bu-Ayesha is my name."

"Thank you, Salem. You should go now before they see you. You might get your family into trouble. Go now, I'll see you again," Sidi Rajab said before waving me off.

When I returned to the tent, Mum and Aisha were sitting together holding hands. I was afraid of my mother's reaction as I knew that they must have seen me.

"Come here, my boy. You're brave like your father. What you did earlier on was a great deed, my son," Mum said while hugging me. "Just be careful. We need you, Salem, but you are truly a hero."

"I'm proud of you, brother," Aisha said breaking her silence. She was always like that; she only spoke when she was spoken to.

The next morning, I went straight to see if Sidi Rajab was still there. I was relieved when I saw the poles empty. I did not see Sidi Rajab for couple of weeks after that but my friend Bubaker came to visit and this time the lump on his head had grown to be quite large.

"Are you okay, Bubaker?" I asked, worrying about the size of his head.

"I am fine apart from this wound. It won't go away. It's getting worse. Anyway, Sidi Rajab doesn't stop talking about you. He said there's a brave boy in the other section of the camp."

I was really worried about him because half of his face was swollen. Even when I told him about my story with the black soldier, he could not laugh because he was in so much pain. But he commented that I am not just a hero but also a trouble maker.

"Listen to me, Bubaker, you have to do something about your wound."

"I'll see Sidi Rajab this evening and maybe he can do something," Bubaker answered. Then he said goodbye and added that his mother was not feeling well. She really took the loss of her parents very badly and was still grieving. I observed Bubaker as he walked behind the tents. He always seemed to be carefree. Later on in life, however, I learned that wars and tragedies could turn a child into a man overnight.

When I returned, Mum and Aisha were sweeping along with other women. This was the only way to make the time pass. In Al-agaila, if you started to think about your misfortune or if you started to cry, you die and you die alone. The Italian soldiers always walked around half-naked this aggravated the men and women of the camp because it was an indecent act. The crude and profane words became the official language of the soldiers. I often watched them and they seemed to be very healthy and happy and did not have a care in the world. Sometimes I wondered how they could be like that when we all live in the same place!

Misery became commonplace in the camp and everyday someone lost a parent, friend, grandfather, grandmother, a daughter, sister, son or a wife. The death cart was always on the move. I always watched the sunset because it was the dawning of a new day that we thought, or possibly wished, that might bring us hope. Yet, day after day we were disappointed when salvation would not come and soon we all lost hope while being treated like animals behind barbwire.

* * *

The following day, we were queuing for dinner. The food was almost inedible, but we ate it against our will because it was the food we waited for all day long. It was a matter of survival, and as my mother always said, hunger is the best sauce. I noticed Sidi Rajab and his wife, Amina, standing in the queue ahead of us.

"Mum, there is Sidi Rajab, the one I told you about. He's with his wife. Can I go and talk to them?" I asked my mother, putting on a face that would be hard for her to refuse.

"I guess so, but just be careful."

"I will," I said with a big smile. I walked up to them and greeted Sidi Rajab and his wife.

"Hello, Sidi Rajab. Hello, Amina."

"Ah, Salem, my little friend. How good to see you," Sidi Rajab replied before turning to his wife. "This is Salem, the brave kid I told you about."

Then the wife turned her attention to me. "Nice to meet you, Salem. Everyone talks about you in our section," Amina said.

"Well, we are there behind you," I told her before I returned to Mum and Aisha. My mother and Amina waved to each other from the distance.

Once we got our share of food, Sidi Rajab and his wife were waiting for us.

"Mrhaba, I'm Amina, and this is my husband, Rajab," Amina introduced herself and her husband while she shook hands with my mother.

"Mrhaba, I am Kalthoum and this is my daughter, Aisha, and I guess you know Salem by now," Mum replied.

"Now that the introduction's out of the way, why don't you come and have your food in our tent to get to know each other better?" Sidi Rajab suggested.

"Thank you. Salem says that you live in the other section. Our tent is only few metres away. Why don't you come over? At least the food will be still hot," my mother said.

"Very well then, your tent it is," Sidi Rajab replied. It was wise to come to our tent anyway as we only lived around the bunkhouse. We all walked to the tent and formed a circle once inside and began eating our food.

"Our only son is fighting along with Sidi Omar. Rajab wanted to join him, but Sidi Omar wouldn't take the two of them together. I need him. Women need their husbands in the mountains," Amina said.

"Yes, it's important to have a man around in times like this and Salem is our man." Mum elaborated further, "My husband, Hassan, and my brother Saleh, are both fighters with Sidi Omar. Sidi Muftah, my father–in–law was with us but tragically we lost him during the march," my mother whimpered.

"Please have mercy. Don't vex your heart. What happened was unacceptable, but you have Salem and Aisha. They need you more than ever." Amina was supportive. I tried to change the mood so I asked Sidi Rajab about the death cart, and where do they bury the bodies?

"Well, son, when a person is dead, the most dignified thing we can offer is to bury them and that's what we do," Sidi Rajab said. "Don't try to grow up too quickly. There are a lot of years ahead of you and there's so much that life will reveal. Only people like us who lived in the gutter and dungeons will appreciate the grace of the Lord, no matter how little."

"Sidi Rajab, you know Bubaker? He was here the other day and he didn't look so well. His wound is getting worse. Please help him, he has no one except you. His mother is sick. He talks about you all the time." I hoped Sidi Rajab would be able to offer some assistance.

"That is very good of you, Salem, to be so thoughtful at that age, but believe me, son, I did everything I could for him. We need more than what we have. They don't care. I think they want us all to die," Sidi Rajab answered angrily. "Look, Salem, look around you, who do you see? Only the most vulnerable and weak: women, old men, kids and babies. The young and strong are with Sidi Omar. In every tent there is someone suffering and there are at least fifty people buried every day. They know, they can see it, but they wouldn't do anything about it simply because they want us to vanish," Sidi Rajab explained to us the sheer scale of the tragedy. Then the shouting of the men in charge started as a sign that it was time for everyone to return to their tents. Sidi Rajab and Amina thanked us for having them in our tent and insisted that the next time we eat, it will be in their tent. Sidi Rajab insisted before leaving.

We slept like chickens here and went to bed at nightfall. Sidi Rajab told me to go to bed early and he promised to bring me to see Bubaker. My mother, Aisha, and Amina exchanged goodbyes. The shouting was getting louder for everyone to sleep. I do not think Mum ever had a full night's sleep. When we are young, we take our parents for granted, but I was crying for them because I felt the love that they had for me. As I grew older and have my own, my love for them increased in size also. It was only then, when I realised the suffering and pain that my mother had gone through, especially in the circumstances we experienced. I felt her pain every time I held my child, and all my life I learned that the only pure and unconditional love is the love for our children.

That night I dreamt about my father coming to us. I dreamt that he was fighting the soldiers and freeing us from this horrible place. The next few days passed and there was no sign of either Sidi Rajab or Bubaker. I was more than concerned. The screaming of women being lashed with whips and the using of profane language from the soldiers became an everyday occurrence. The men were moving the dirt from one place to another. It now seemed endless. I went to the steps of the bunkhouse and sat there. I took what was left of my shoe off and I started putting a piece of cardboard into it and watched the Italian soldiers in the watchtower.

In a trice, I saw Sidi Rajab walking behind the death cart. He seemed lost in his thoughts and without any delay, I ran to him barefoot as my shoe was in my hand.

"Mrhaba, Sidi Rajab," I greeted him while walking.

"Mrhaba, Salem. Don't let them see you, son. Go now, I'll come to you later. Go on," Sidi Rajab replied very quickly.

That evening we were sitting around our mother and she told us one of her most interesting tales about the ghoul and the dwarf before the voice of Amina drew our attention to the front of the tent.

"Kalthoum, are you there?" she asked.

"Mrhaba, Amina, I'm coming," Mum said. Amina entered the tent and my mother greeted her with the traditional Bedouin salutation.

"It's Bubaker; he's in a very serious condition." After she said this, those words had a profound effect on me and it felt like I had just been stabbed with a knife. "Salem," she called out.

"Yes, Aunty Amina?" I answered politely.

"Rajab is waiting for you outside. Go to him, son," Amina told me in a low voice.

"Oh, Lord give us patience," my mother commented.

"It's the only remedy available in this place, and thank God it doesn't come in a box," Amina added. I ran out of the tent and there was Sidi Rajab, stroking his beard with his left hand.

"Salem, my son, come. Bubaker is very sick and he wants to see you. You must come with me at once," Sidi Rajab said and seemed in a hurry.

"I will tell my mother that I'm going with you. I won't be long," I replied while getting back to the tent. Within minutes, Sidi Rajab and I were moving between the tents very quickly in order to avoid the soldiers. Once we were outside Bubaker's tent, Sidi Rajab made a sound like clearing his throat to alert the women inside.

Then Khadija shouted from inside the tent, "Come in. Bubaker's waiting for you."

We entered and it was a bit dark. The women moved back to make space for us. There were lots of children there surrounding Bubaker.

"Come, Salem, get closer," Bubaker said in a very weak voice. We both sat beside him. His head was covered but the swelling was very noticeable. His face was also completely black and blue and his left eye completely shut.

"Sorry, Salem, for not coming to you. I tried but couldn't lift my head. Sidi Rajab had a look at it earlier on," Bubaker informed me.

"It's okay. Just get better,?" I replied knowing that the worst was yet to come, but I masked my concerns by putting on a brave face. Then Bubaker managed a smile and asked me about my battered shoes.

We chatted for a while and I promised that I would come and visit him. We wished each other well and a good night's sleep before Sidi Rajab and I were moving like thieves in the darkness.

Once we got to our tent, Sidi Rajab said, "If you need anything, please come to us. Salem knows now where to find us." Then left with his wife.

That night I did not fall asleep instantly. I was looking at the tent roof thinking about Bubaker and his poor mother. The morbid sounds of mothers weeping and the endless cries of agony began. Heavy pounding of army boots, people quarrelling and Italian soldiers singing also added to the cacophony of sounds lingering around us. This was what we had to endure every night in the Camp of Suffering.

CHAPTER NINE

A quandary is where we live now and only the Lord could save us from it. One old woman told us that while she was queuing for the morning tea. It was in this queue that people heard stories from others. People were still coming out of their tents like columns of ants except that they had neither the ant's energy nor enthusiasm of looking forward to the day. Every day was like a week and every week was like a month, and every month a year.

The soldiers released those who got punished the previous night to have their tea and to resume their work. It was another day in Al-agaila and business as usual. The death cart was a constant reminder of death's grip on the camp. There was nothing on my mind except the words of Bubaker making fun of my shoe and the smile that he managed despite his condition. I must say that I started to hate that cart, and I even thought of burning the wretched thing, but when I shared the idea with Aisha, she told me that would not change anything. Death was still going to be there and another cart would be made to replace it. Aisha also made me promise not to do anything daft.

In the distance I could see that dreadful death cart appear with men bearing sad faces walking behind it. They walked slowly and their faces and demeanour were of fatigue. The unmistakable frame of Sidi Rajab was walking taller than the rest. Without thinking and without any regard for Mum and Aisha, I found myself running toward him. He saw me coming and tried to stop me by shaking his head, but I kept running until I was standing beside him. Sidi Rajab told me to go at once. I stood like a soldier, obeying his commander and I was about to turn. Instantly I felt a heavy object strike my back. After the blow, it felt as if every bone in my back was broken. Mergigo, the black soldier who we nicknamed because he was so skinny, was the one who hit me. I felt the pain, but I managed to run and he christened me with every name under the sun. I must say that I was laughing about the whole thing, later on when my mother massaged my back she didn't find it very amusing and she was cross with me for not listening, but her anger soon abated.

It had been three days since Sidi Rajab came to see me about Bubaker. On the fourth day, Sidi Rajab came alone and he was carrying something in his hand.

"Assalamu Alykoum," Sidi Rajab greeted me. He looked so depressed and downtrodden.

"Wa alaikum alsalam," we all replied almost simultaneously. Mum held my hand as she knew what he was about to say. "What have you brought, Sidi Rajab?"

"Here, Salem, this is for you. Bubaker wanted you to have them." Sidi Rajab handed me a pair of black boots.

"Why, did he get new ones?" I asked.

"No, Salem. I'm sorry to say that Bubaker passed away in the early hours of this morning and that's why I didn't want you to come near the cart because his body was there," Sidi Rajab explained in a soft and sympathetic voice. I could not control my feelings. I shouted with tears drowning my eyes.

"No, Bubaker must still be there! He promised to have a game with us. He can't go without telling me," I cried. Aisha and Mum were crying also.

I ran out of the tent. Sidi Rajab tried to hold me but I needed to go. I wanted to run and never stop. I wanted to go to his tent. Sidi Rajab followed me and he took me into his arms. I cried until I was no longer able to. I never forgot Bubaker. He was an amazing boy and I learned a lot from him. Even though our friendship was short, it was full of meaning. He knew I needed a shoe and even on his deathbed, he thought of me. When I did not see Bubaker again in the camp, I knew he was gone, never to return. The next day I put the boots on. They were heavy and big with no laces but they were tough and did the job for the whole period that I spent there. The day that did not kill you in Al-agaila, certainly made you tougher and more resilient.

The urination and defecation was still a major problem for the men and women but for us it became fun. Every time nature called, we stood facing the watchtowers, took out our little penises and pissed on the buildings. The next day I took my old shoes and walked straight to the death cart and threw my shoes into it. The men looked at me and probably wondered why I did something like that. I smiled and told them that my shoe was dead. They all smiled back, but only Sidi Rajab understood what I meant.

In the days that followed, I got to know all the soldiers (both Italians and Arterians) by name. Around this time I also begun learning Italian by repeating the words and the Italian soldiers answered me back, sometimes correcting my mistakes. I also disobeyed the law by going near the red line, which was getting closer to the wires. They followed me a lot but they got tired of me. They thought I was a worthless little brat that posed no threat to them. I got to know Marco, Motto and Sergio.

It was not long before Sidi Rajab approached my mother. "Listen, Kalthoum, Salem is a clever kid and we need him to help our people, especially the babies and the elderly."

"But how? In the name of God, he's only a child!" Mum said with disdain.

"By getting him to get inside the bunkhouse, the canteen and storeroom. Salem can do it and I have a plan," Sidi Rajab explained.

"Forgive me, but I will never risk my boy. Hassan will never forgive me for that. Please don't put any more weight over the one I'm already carrying. He's only eight years old, for heavens sake?" Mum replied, her voice wavering and on the brink of crying.

"Don't upset yourself, Kalthoum. I do understand and I know how you feel. I probably would react the same way if Salem was my son. Please forgive me for bringing this up." Sidi Rajab bowed in an apologetic manner and asked his wife to get ready to leave. I did not sleep that night. I was thinking of everything that Sidi Rajab told Mum.

Weeks passed and by the end of November, the nights became unbearable as the furious and unforgiving desert winter loomed, bringing with it cold howling winds. The harsh winter took its toll on people and the dead were no longer counted. After few days, when the weather settled a bit, I went to the other section. I made a promise to Bubaker that we would have a game of hide and seek. I gathered all the children and told them that this game was for Bubaker. We played all day and all the time I felt that Bubaker was with us.

After few weeks had elapsed, the provisions trucks made extra deliveries to the camp. African mercenaries were first to receive it and took the load straight into the storerooms, which were situated behind the bunkhouse. Sometimes they arrived in the evenings when Sidi Rajab and Amina came to visit.

"I curse those ruthless people. Look at all the provisions they bring: drinks, vegetables, dry meat and cheese! You name it and it's there, and what they feed us even animals wouldn't dare eat," Sidi Rajab stated, seething and unable to contain his frustration.

"Yeah, they're very mean. We're hungry and they don't even care," I replied.

"I am still determined to get into the storerooms and ammunition store. This is the only way we can help the sick, the weak and Sidi Omar's men," Sidi Rajab said. I must say that the idea was the only way to stay alive, but my mother would die before seeing me getting caught.

"I'd do it, but you know I would be breaking my promise to my mother and I can't do that," I said in a round–about way of telling them that I was not yet ready to carry out that task.

"Please, son," Sidi Rajab pleaded, "try to keep everything we said between ourselves. I'll see you later." He moved off vigilantly. Sidi Rajab came back with a swag. He took it out from underneath his cloak where it was hidden. He handed it to his wife, "This is all we got this week," Sidi Rajab whispered.

"Wait, I have to give you my share," my mother said and took a small bag with pieces of hard, stale bread. I did not understand what was going on at first, but later Sid Rajab explained the whole thing to me. I was so surprised and amazed at people's willpower. Everyone gave small share of their daily bread or whatever could be eaten and by the end of the week,

Sidi Rajab and other men gave it to Sidi Omar's men through the barbwire. I got so excited that I went out and surreptitiously collected small stones. I went near the watchtower and hid behind a tent and started pelting the soldiers with them. There were two of them. At first I could not aim right and then I could not get the power that I wanted to maximise the impact. After many attempts and misses, I finally got it right and they were deadly. The soldiers were screaming in agony, scanning the area underneath them, but were unsuccessful as I found myself a good hiding place. One yelled at the top of his lungs, "*Quella sue negro cazzo*", blaming the African soldiers. The other one vowed to shoot the bastard responsible. The enjoyment was beyond description.

In the evening we were queuing for the usual slop we called dinner. The sordid womaniser, Colonel Brachi, made an appearance. He was an ugly bastard with a large potbelly and a big baldhead. He often came out in the evening holding a bottle of wine. I got to know all this from Sidi Rajab. He told me that it was alcohol and it made you drunk. The colonel was standing on the steps of the bunkhouse, checking all the women with lustful eyes. Brachi was not just content with doing this, but he would scream crude obscenities at the women. His soldiers laughed and cheered every time he opened his mouth. We all hated him because he was a sleazy, horrible creature. My mother always hid Aisha, who wore her headscarf all the time.

Back at the tent, my mother was busy stitching her own boots, which bore the signs of a battering. Aisha and I were playing "Giran", some old traditional game that was played by using five small stones. Then we heard the unmistakable cough of Sidi Rajab trying to alert the women that a man is nearby. It was like knocking at the door before entering someone's room, except we had no door in our tent. It was unusual to see another woman coming with Amina at this hour. I thought that something must have happened. I was delighted to see Sidi Rajab. After the greeting and salutations, all the women sat and formed a circle and then Amina whispered something into my mother's ear. Aisha and I waited for our mother's reaction. Then Sid Rajab spoke.

"Listen, Kalthoum, you're a strong woman and you believe in Allah." Before he finished, my mother started crying and the women, too. Then Sidi Rajab continued, "Strengthen your spine, Kalthoum. Your husband Hassan has passed away." He then concluded by saying, "We all belong to Allah and to him we shall return."

Aisha and I ran to our mother and hugged her. We cried with her and the women gave Mum words of sympathy and support. I still did not understand what was going on.

"What happened to my father?" I asked.

"Your father is a martyr, Salem," Sidi Rajab said.

"What does that mean?"

"Your father died fighting the Italians. He died fighting for his country," Sidi Rajab explained.

"No, my father's not dead. My father always keeps his promises. He told me he'd come for me. No, my father will be back!"

"Come, my son." Sidi Rajab took me into his arms. "You have to be proud of your father. He died freeing his country."

I refused to come to terms with the idea that my father was gone from this world forever. I was angry with him because he promised me that dawn when we prayed together that he would come back to take me hunting with him.

"Please, Salem, calm down, your father is a hero and that's how you should always remember him." Sidi Rajab desperately tried to make me come to terms with the fact that my father was no longer in this world. Mum and Aisha were crying and so too were the other women. My mother then composed herself and was strong for us.

"How and when did this happen?" Mum asked showing total acceptance.

"It was a few weeks ago, but the news didn't reach us until last week, but I couldn't inform you then until we got confirmation of his death. He died along with Sidi Al-Fadeel Bu–Omar," Sidi Rajab said, and then he started reciting some verse from the Quran. Once Mum, Aisha and the other women heard the name of Sidi Al-Fadeel, they wept again. Sidi Rajab continued to explain how it happened and how the men were so brave. They were only a few men fighting an armed Italian unit.

"Your father did not suffer, Salem, and died very quickly. Your mother and sister need you now more than ever so wipe away your tears and come with me," Sidi Rajab said. I held his hand as we went for a walk. Once we got outside the tent, I cried with all my heart.

"Cry, Salem, let the tears wash your heart. Cry with all your heart and let the tears wash away your sadness. We will never cherish the moments of embrace if we never lived the minutes of departure." Sidi Rajab made me feel good, but our grieving really began when everyone left. We consoled each other. At night we all hugged one another and cried.

Then Aisha spoke, "We shouldn't be too sad. Dad told me that martyrs don't die. Maybe he's still around looking out for us." Her words made me feel so good. I liked the idea that my father was still there watching over us.

At dawn, I was standing outside the tent. Everything was so quiet and then it started to rain. I raised my head and I let the rain wash off my face. It had not been washed in a long time. I thought the sky was crying because it mourned my father's departure from this world..

That night, my mother was preparing me for something, she faced me when she started her conversation. "Salem, my son, despite all the pain and suffering that we're going through inside here, we are united, we're one big family. Your father was a brave man, a man who loved his country so much. Your father fought the Italians so that we would have a home again. Those invaders have no reason, no cause to stay or to be here in the first place and certainly have no right to treat us like this. Do you know, Salem that Sidi Rajab has lost three sons? They all died on the battlefield. But look at him, how strong and determined he is, but believe me, Salem, he's grieving for them in his own way. he must be strong because he knows that we need strong men and women like him. He knows that if he crumbles, then a lot of people will fall. I loved your father so much and I'll grieve for him as long as I live, but I must live for you. We need to be strong to survive this death trap. Always remember, Salem, that patience, time and faith are the only weapons that can get you through everything. I love you, Salem, and I love you, Aisha." My mother then kissed our foreheads and hugged us.

December's bitter winterish weather snuck deep into our bones and the night winds of the desert howled like a hungry wolf, but we were extra warm as my grandfather's cloak came in very handy. My mother shivered in fear every time she heard the soldiers' footsteps passing by our tent. She prayed every time she heard them shouting or singing. Mum took Aisha deep into her bosom every night.

The camp's population was dwindling by the day. New faces came to our section: Drees, Yousef and Ayoub. They were the three orphans who had been re–located with other families. They were around my age and now my new friends. Even in Al-agaila, sometimes you smiled and thanked the Lord because you knew that you were luckier than the rest and that your misery and misfortune were nothing compared to the tragedies of others.

CHAPTER TEN

Everyone in the camp was experiencing heartache of some kind. Clouds gathered in the sky and there was a little drizzle, but also a chill in the air. Something unusual was happening in the camp that attracted the attention of everyone and gave people something to talk about. They were preparing for some sort of celebration, but I did not know what. One optimistic old man said that they were celebrating our release.

"Wishful thinking," a very old woman quipped when she heard his remark.

"People haven't lost their wit. I'll give them that," Sidi Rajab remarked while we stood in the queue for dinner.

The soldiers worked all day long putting up the Italian flag on top of the watchtowers, the bunkhouse, even on top of our tents and they brought hundreds of lanterns and placed them around the camp.

"They're celebrating Christmas," Sidi Rajab told me.

"What is Christmas anyway?" I asked.

"Well, Christmas is the celebration of the birth of the prophet Jesus. Peace be upon him."

The next day a big truck arrived with more supplies. There was everything from fresh fruits to boxes of vegetables and even cigarettes. They even brought so many turkeys and many boxes of different kind of bottles. Sidi Rajab explained to me about those boxes when I asked him and he said that it was alcoholic drinks. He also said that it makes people lose their minds when they drank it.

"Why do they do that if it's that bad?" I enquired. He paused for a second and then smiled before answering.

"That's the reason they do it, simply to lose their minds, escape reality for a while."

That evening Sidi Rajab was talking to a young man and he called me over. "Ah, Salem. Come, my son. This is Nuri. He's from Benghazi."

Sidi Nuri introduced himself and then it was my turn. "Hello, my name is Salem. I am here with my mother and sister."

"Salem lost his grandfather during the march and also lost his father. The news came a few weeks ago. He died fighting the Italians in the mountain," Sidi Rajab explained.

"I'm sorry for your loss. Everyone has suffered here," Nuri answered. I was surprised to see a man Nuri's age here. Most people in the camp were either old or very young.

"Nuri has lost twenty members of his immediate family in here," Sidi Rajab said.

"Twenty? How? I'm so sorry." I truly was shocked. I did not know what to say. I guess Sidi Rajab mentioned that to make me forget my pain when I heard what Nuri had to go through. Only later did I learn that Nuri's entire family brought here as a punishment for something they did not do, and in their short stay in Al-agaila they were subjected to all sorts of torture. In a cruel and ironic twist of fate, only when his entire family were killed, the Italians discovered that they were innocent.

"Are you from Albtnan?" Nuri asked.

"No. I'm from the Green Mountain," I replied. Nuri's tragedy was a reflection of what occurred inside the camp. We were still talking when I noticed some other children talking to each other between the tents and their heads were looking in every direction. My instincts told me that they are up to something, so I excused myself from Sidi Rajab and Nuri and went to investigate.

I ran to the boys and once I got to them, their faces lit up with delight. They were certainly happy to see me.

"Hi, Salem, how are you?" Drees asked while scratching his head.

"I'm very well, thank you. What's that in your hand?" I asked curiously.

"Oh, this is a sling, I mean a sling shot," Drees answered. This time he scratched under his arm.

"Well, I can hit that guard on that tower from here using only my hand," I said and it unintentionally sounded boastful.

"We heard a lot of good things about you, Salem, but never a braggart," Ayoub said.

"I didn't mean to brag," I replied and scolded myself for sounding so self–assured.

"Don't mind him, Salem, he's a teaser." Yousef came to my defence. "Well, you can hit things with your hand, but that needs a lot of patience and practice. With this little beauty, you can be sure that you'll hit your target all the time," Drees insisted. I must say that I was a bit excited and many devilish ideas came rushing into my head. Then I remembered Mergigo when I hit him hard and he started jumping like a crazy man. I could not stop laughing.

"What are you laughing about?" Drees asked.

"No, nothing. I didn't mean to be rude. I just remembered something funny," I replied before recounting to them the tale of hitting Mergigo and the Italian guard and how they had a go at each other. The boys laughed.

"This is really funny, Salem. I have to give you my sling," Drees insisted.

"Thank you very much, but I couldn't take it."

"I insist. I can make another one. Please take it, I want you to have it," Drees insisted while sticking his hand inside his Jalabiya and scratched his back.

"Are you suffering from some sort of rash?" I asked while accepting the sling.

"Who hasn't got a rash in this bloody place? Soon you will have one yourself."

We all laughed and arranged to meet the next day to have a go at the guards with our new toys. I was admiring my new weapon. Once the boys left, I turned around and there was Sidi Rajab saying goodbye to Nuri. Then he came straight to me.

"What is this in your hand, Salem?" Sidi Rajab questioned firmly.

"It's a sling. Drees gave it to me. He makes them himself," I told him.

"Listen, there's a lot of talk between the guards and they are blaming each other, but I know it's you who's doing it, isn't it?"

"Yes, Sidi Rajab, it was me." There was no point in lying or denying it as this man knew me too well.

"You're not just brave and clever, but also an honest kid. Imagine Salem what will happen if you got caught. They will come down heavy on you and it will break the hearts of both your mother and Aisha," Sidi Rajab reminded me.

"I won't let anyone down, I promise," I vowed to him.

"Good. Before you were doing it alone, now you have more children around. If one acts foolishly, everyone will get blamed," Sidi Rajab said. Then he bid me goodnight and told me to go straight home. He said he had few tents to visit and things to do.

After Sidi Rajab left, I ran my hand down along the body of the sling and if I'm to be honest, it was very tempting to use. I was so glad that I told him the truth. My father always said that lies have a short age. Telling the truth is also a form of bravery and makes the truthful trustworthy. The shouting of the guards began telling people that it was time to sleep. As soon as I entered our tent, I saw Aisha combing my mother's hair. I greeted them and with a big smile and they greeted me back.

In Al-agaila, every day was the same, bringing the same misery and tears. However, one morning a lot of things occurred. There was the arrival of new soldiers and the departure of others. Sidi Rajab explained the reason for this stating that they exchanged guards to give the married soldiers a chance to spend Christmas with their families, but he expressed some concern. He said that normally the new guards would be young or unmarried and they could be reckless. Also something horrible occurred on that morning. There was a lot of commotion and mayhem. The whole camp was there to witness this act of indecency and degradation. Five women were pulled by their hair from their tents and dragged along the ground by their legs and arms. They were hopelessly screaming for help. They were followed by their children, husbands, or relations, but no one could come to their rescue. The soldiers used their guns to push back the men and the mercenaries used whips and sticks. Then the soldiers ripped the women's clothes, exposing their private parts, and the unfortunate women were pushed to the ground. Their hands and legs were tied on small sticks dug deep into the ground. To add to this heartlessness, they received many lashes and with every lash our hearts sunk even further. We stood there helpless and felt useless. The guards were cheering and laughing, making horrible gestures. It was a sad day. The children and women were crying and men felt like they wanted the earth to split open and swallow them, as they felt worthless. My mother held the two of us in her hands. She was crying, and prayed to God to end this atrocity and degradation. The women were left there for many hours. Sidi Rajab and other men took their coats and covered them. That was the only heroic thing they could do.

The crowd was quickly dispersed. I sought answers but only later I discovered the devastating truth of the screaming of women by night and the punishment they got by day.

Sidi Rajab was right again as those new soldiers were dirtier and so malicious. They were drinking outside the bunkhouse day and night, fighting, wrestling and shouting. My mother's concerns increased as the days passed.

Queuing for food become unbearable and something, no one looked forward to as the soldiers become more aggressive and intimidating. The colonel was always there, like a beast singling out his prey and waiting for the right moment to pounce on it.

"This sordid, dirty womaniser will soon burn in hell," Sidi Rajab said. I could tell he was seething. All women were taking extra care, covering their faces and the faces of their daughters with their headscarves.

"May God protect us from the evil ones," Mum muttered.

"May Allah hear your prayers, Kalthoum," Amina added. To me, it seemed like all the women were constantly on edge. Sidi Rajab and his wife were always with us in the queue. The atmosphere around the camp was disastrous approaching Christmas. Several men discussed about putting in a complaint to the colonel, but Sidi Rajab refuted them. He told them,

"Going to the colonel to complain is like asking for mercy from the executioner, and you damn well know that complaining is a crime in this place and you get punished for it. So save yourselves and be extra vigilant as the hard days are still to come."

As we were returning with our grub to the tent, Sidi Rajab got closer to me and spoke very quietly. "Listen, Salem, your mum and Aisha need you more than ever now."

I must say that Sidi Rajab's words made me age ten years in one day. That night I went behind our tent and cried. I was angry with my grandfather and my father. I was still unable to understand how they left and without telling me. When I was younger, I always thought that they lived forever and when I learned to count, I often said to my father,

"When I am one hundred years old, you will be an old man."

When I entered the tent, Mum and Aisha were talking but stopped as soon as they saw me.

"Alsalamou Alykoum," I said greeting them.

"Wa Alaikum As Salam," both replied.

"Where did you go, my son, at this hour?" Mum asked worryingly.

"I was behind the tent watching all the lanterns. They look good at night and it makes the camp look different," I answered.

"I saw your friends today, Salem. They were playing with their slings and they were aiming at an empty can," Aisha said.

"Damn! I told them not to be doing that. They could get us into trouble. I'll talk to them in the morning," I replied, infuriated.

"Does that mean you carry one as well, Salem?"

"Yes, Mum," I answered taking the sling out from under my Jalabiya.

"Oh, Salem, you want to kill me before my time! Hand it to me. I'll hide it for you," Mum said. Then I sat and told them my story about the Italians and Areterians and how Mergigo was squealing like a rat, barking like a dog and jumping like someone with a scorpion in his pants. I told them about the Italian guard and how he lost his temper and threatened to kill all the black soldiers and how he was swearing while waving his hands. Mum and Aisha laughed like they had never laughed before. We guffawed so loud that sometimes we had to put our hands over our mouths. This was the first time we laughed since we came to the Camp of Suffering. In Al-agaila you could lose your smile if you lost hope.

Aisha showered me with praise. "You're not just a brave brother but also very funny."

That night Mum told us everything about our father and Uncle Saleh and all the time that they were away, they were not really working as she used to tell us but instead going to their camp to fight the Italians along with Sidi Omar. I closed my eyes and started imagining that I was fighting the soldiers here with my mighty sling and making them scream and flee. I imagined walking back home with all the people in the concentration camp. But those blood–curdling screams of young girls and the weeping of women haunted my ears, banishing my beautiful dreams.

CHAPTER ELEVEN

That night when we all laughed, it was a night of mixed emotions, but like my mother often told me, "That's life." In the morning, she put on her boots to start her daily work with other women of the section. I was yawning, stretching and scratching my hair at the same time while standing outside the tent. The days were getting shorter.

The weather was permanently dull in the month of December and an invasion of black clouds in the sky proved that rain was imminent. All this miserable weather contributed to the gloomy feeling around the camp. Sidi Rajab was walking behind the death cart collecting the corpses of those who lost their lives the night before. He seemed lost in his thoughts. I waved to him and he waved back to me. The black soldiers were busy bringing big pots from the storeroom to the yard and making the fire spots by putting big stones in circles for the pots to be positioned on. They had assigned more men and women to gather wood and were marched toward the gate escorted by armed Italian soldiers.

By the afternoon the steam rose high from the boiling pots. A turkey was brought out from the back of the bunkhouse, where it had been kept for the last couple of weeks. It seemed to have gotten bigger. Obviously they were fattening them for the occasion. All the prisoners of the camp felt wronged, as the birds were fed to gain weight while we were left starving and to die a slow death.

"What is all the fuss about? We're both facing the same fate," an elderly woman said as she stood outside her tent holding her cane with both hands. It was a weird looking bird that I have never seen before, but the weirdest thing was the way the black soldiers were killing them in a gruesome manner. They were hitting the birds on the head, and once they lost consciousness, they broke their neck with their hands and then went straight into the hot boiling pots. A few minutes later, they took them out and put them on big aluminium trays and the women who were assigned for that work started plucking the plumage. Not long before the bird was completely bald, the black soldiers carried it inside like carrying a new born baby. The kids and I looked on with a great deal of curiosity. It was something we had never seen before.

Everyone was dreaming of good food that night and a scrumptious hot meal, unfortunately for us, that night we received the same as before. We had boiling water with the taste of onion and feathers, which is all we got from that turkey. We had never received any meat since arriving at that camp. The five of us went back to our tent.

"The poor peoples' food is the best food. Do you know why, Salem?" Sidi Rajab asked.

"Sorry, Sidi Rajab, I can't think of any good reason," I answered. Everyone smiled at the response I gave.

"Salem, you're still young and this hard bread tastes delicious in our mouths, better than the king's food. Do you know why, son?" He took a sip from his cup.

"Is it because we're starving?" I again replied in a witty tone. This time Aisha, Mum and Amina giggled.

"No, son, because we eat our food after a hard day's work under the beating sun, the freezing weather or the lashing rain. That's why, Salem," Sidi Rajab answered while taking a feather out of his mouth.

My mother smiled and said, "We thank God for everything. The most important thing for me is that you and Aisha are safe and healthy."

"We are suffering, but we still have faith in God. Sometimes too much of a luxurious life can distance you from the Lord," Amina added.

"The other day I heard an old man saying that sleep is food for the poor. Is that true, Sidi Rajab?" I asked.

"Well, that depends on whether you can sleep on an empty stomach or not," Sidi Rajab answered with a smile. We all laughed. "It's the dreams of the poor that disperse the sleep of the tyrant," Sidi Rajab remarked. We talked some more, reflecting on the last six months, and remembered those who died. Then Sidi Rajab and Amina went back to their tent. We had a rather quiet night. There was not much activity going on around us and only the whistling of the wind was all that could be heard.

The next morning the air in the camp was brimming with an assortment of different aromas. This was surely not good for us because it made things harder. Yet we were still optimistic and we had not lost faith in good hot food and nicely baked fresh bread. I mean, after all, as Sidi Rajab said, dreams are free and there was no harm in being positive. However, that evening brought further disappointment for us. As soldiers were preparing their food, they completely forgot about us. We received nothing that evening. People aired their complaints to the soldiers, but normally their response was with the sticks and whips on our backs. They told us to go to our tents with our tails between our legs, leaving us angry, frustrated and hungry.

Christmas Day was the worst in terms of food because we did not even get a crumb. When we got back to the tent, Mum took a small swag that she hid pieces of bread from her share to give it to Sidi Rajab for the men of Sid Omar. She opened the swag and said that it was nothing, but would get us through the night. We all reached out our hands and took a small piece from it. As we were biting on the very hard bread, our eyes welled up.

That night the soldiers were singing and shouting and what made it worse, was the singing of the black soldiers, which was more like squealing. Each of them were telling the other to shut up and blaming each other for their disgraceful singing. Obviously, they ate and drank a lot.

People were out at the break of dawn wearing their cloaks around their body as the weather started getting colder during the day, but there was no sign of the soldiers on the ground in our section except those in the towers. Men and women went about their daily routine but without the bustle of soldiers' activity. It was almost noon before the soldiers awoke and they looked terrible.

The next few days passed at a snail's pace. Sounds of thunder came from time to time, but it seemed like it came from a distance. One afternoon the delivery truck arrived bringing more food and extra supplies of alcohol and cigarettes. They were preparing for the New Year, the night that Sidi Rajab dreaded the most. Then it arrived. Soldiers commenced their festivities in the morning, while drinking heavily all day. An uneasy feeling dwelled amongst us.

I had not seen my friends for almost a week. I thought that Sidi Rajab might have had a word or two with them to not come near me, especially when my mother told him that I handed her my sling. Mum granted me permission to go and visit them. It was not long before I spotted Ayoub standing, chatting with two girls.

The minute he saw me he shouted, "Mrhaba, Salem. What brings you here?"

"Mrhaba, Ayoub. Well, I haven't seen you in a while so I got a bit worried and I came over," I answered.

"This is Khadija and Fatima, they're sisters. They live in that tent over there."

They were beautiful girls and they were our age. We exchanged greetings and then Ayoub turned his attention to me, "Yes, where were we? Ah, the reason we haven't been able to come to you is that Yousef and Drees have lost some relatives and they have to be there to look after the old," Ayoub explained.

"That's too bad. I'd like to go and see them. Can we go to them?"

"Yes indeed, they'll be very happy to see you, Salem," Ayoub replied enthusiastically. We said goodbye to the girls and made our way to Drees and Yousef. Once we got there, Yousef and Drees were so happy to see me. We talked about everything that happened in the last week and I told them that we had to forget about the slings for a while, explaining the reason why. They were very understanding and promised that they would hide theirs too.

"I have to go. It's getting darker. Goodbye," I said before promising to return the next day. The days were very short so it got dark quite early. I had to rush home before Mum started panicking.

The wind was getting stronger by the minute and it was very cold. That blasted death cart just returned for the last time that day from its many daily trips from outside the camp to bury the dead, also the men in charge of gathering wood retuned with stacks carried over their backs. Everyone seemed in a hurry to return to their tents. In the sky there were flashes of lightning and this injected fear into everyone's heart. This was followed by roaring thunder and the skies opened up.

We ran from the food queue, and by the time we got to our tents we were soaking wet, after drying ourselves off, we ate our food. The thunder's bellowing made me nervous. Aisha, for some reason, seemed to be distant and for the first time I saw sadness in her eyes. Aisha usually did not talk much but that night she was saying things that made me and my mother cry. Aisha was talking like we would never see her again. My mother was edgy when making the bed. Her hands were shaking. She never stopped praying. I heard Amina saying to Mum earlier in the queue that she should be extra vigilant. I wondered if this was the night that my mother dreaded for the last six months. My mother took us in her arms and she said to me that she needed me.

"I'm not afraid, Mama. I just don't want to leave you, that's all," Aisha said while wiping her tears.

"You're not going anywhere, my sweetheart," Mum answered.

Bright flashes of lightning almost lit up the area around us. Thunder roared like a raging monster and the rain pounded on our tent. The shouting and screaming grew louder along with the soldiers' heavy boots stomping on the muddy ground as they marched. Voices of old men begging for mercy joined the shouts. My mother's fears showed and I heard her heart pounding rapidly. It was horrible when you were waiting for something awful to happen. Every time soldiers walked or ran near our tent, the three of us held onto each other tightly. No one dared to sleep.

Singing and cursing from the soldiers became even more boisterous. Many Italians had lost their minds due to the excessive drinking. When they spoke, their words were slurred and incoherent.

Suddenly their shouting was louder than before. The flashes of lightning acted like a spotlight and illuminated the whole place. Through the tent, we could see three silhouettes standing there and instantly we knew they were soldiers. We pretended to be asleep, but then one of them took the cover off. We all got scared but remained lying down. An Italian officer and two black Areterian soldiers looked down at us. The officer had a bottle in his hand. One black soldier carried an oil lamp. The black soldiers' eyes and teeth were the only things I could see. Then he raised the lamp and they looked like three hideous monsters, similar to the ones that my grandfather used to talk about in his stories.

"This is the girl," the Italian said, "take her." As one of the black guards tried to grab Aisha, Mum and I put our hands forward to stop him. Taking another swig from the bottle, the Italian screamed again.

"Please, have mercy on us. I have no one but them!" Mum begged. "Please don't take her. She needs me, please." Her pleas were ignored by the drunk Italian.

"You fucking black bastard, take her," the officer barked, enraged. The black soldier caught Aisha by the arm and he pulled her toward him. Aisha was screaming and Mum and I tried desperately to free her. We cried, begged and screamed. Screams were also coming from everywhere else in the camp. The other soldier stepped in and hit me hard on the arm. I had to let go of Aisha.

"Fucking Bedouin!" the malevolent Italian officer ranted.

"Please leave us alone. She is only a baby, she's thirteen-years-old!" Mum again pleaded while she wept. Aisha whimpered and was like a helpless gazelle in the hands of a pack of hyenas. I launched myself at the men, kicking them anywhere I could.

One black soldier shouted in Italian, "Take this, you stubborn little Bedouin," and then struck me on the forehead with his stick. I stumbled and fell on my back. Something hot ran down my face and before I knew it, I was bleeding.

"Please have mercy! Please, I beg you. Take me. Do whatever you want to me. Please let them go!" Mum beseeched them. Taking one step back and with all his might, the Italian kicked Mum in the stomach. That moment everything went silent. I could hear nothing anymore. It seemed like everything went mute. My mother's face blanched and she desperately gasped for air. I stood up once again and charged at them, unleashing a feral scream. I caught the Italian officer's hand and I sank my teeth into his arm. He squealed like a pig and, catching a fistful of my hair, he pulled me up so hard that a piece of his flesh was in my mouth.

"*Ci cazzo animale!*" Then he kicked me hard in the groin. I was on my knees trying to inhale as much air as I could. Even though everything happened in a couple of minutes, it seemed like a lifetime. Mum and I were helpless as Aisha was dragged away. As they took her away from us, she kept calling my name and I looked into her eyes. I cried while still fighting to get some air into my lungs. Mum wept too. I crawled to the front of the tent and rain fell relentlessly. I stayed there for a minute and raised my hands up to the sky.

"Please help us, God," I shouted, but it was pointless as Aisha was gone. I returned to the tent and put a blanket over Mum's shoulder. She fell into my arms and now I no longer felt like a nine year old. The Camp of Suffering transformed me into a man of ninty.

Morning came and it was dull when I woke up. My body was bruised all over and blood had dried on my forehead and face. My clothes were damp and Mum was missing. I put my boots on and went looking for her. The ground was wet and muddy. My mother was outside the bunkhouse crying, asking people if they had seen her daughter. Soldiers screamed at her to go away. When I got there, one soldier tried to push her but I stood between them. I glared at him with eyes of hatred. He raised his hands and moved back.

"This kid has balls," he said with a sinister laugh. I took Mum by the hand and took her back to our tent. She was crying and said numerous times that Aisha was gone and that she could never forgive herself. I comforted her as best I could.

"It's not your fault, it's their fault. We did everything we could." As I uttered these words, she just stared ahead and seemed lost. My mother was never the same again.

That night Sidi Rajab and his wife, along with other women, came to comfort us. I did not talk to anyone for days and followed my mother around the camp. She asked everyone she met about Aisha. Sometimes I had to walk for miles to find her. My instincts told me that Mum was not well and that kick did not help matters either. She lost interest in everything, even food and water. On many occasions, I had to force her to eat something. She cried by night and wandered around aimlessly by day. Sidi Rajab followed me from a distance. You could say he was like my guardian angel trying to protect me. I had to do something to somehow alleviate Mum's agony. I looked at the soldiers every day with disgust. I was no longer afraid. I wanted my sling back but Sidi Rajab begged me not to do that for the sake of my mother.

Mum did not last long after Aisha was taken away that night. One night she held my hand so tight that she wanted to say something but failed to. She was in a lot of pain. That kick had done more damage than I expected. Mum was bleeding and I wanted to call for help. She did not want help, however and just held my arm, asking me to sit by her side. She shivered and was sweating. At her request, I leaned in closer and she whispered something into my ear. I started crying because Mum was saying goodbye. She asked me to promise her to stay alive and told me that she loved us with all her heart.

"I'm weeping for you, my son. I can no longer go on. Stay closer to Sidi Rajab." Mum kissed my forehead. I slept beside her and I knew she was crying despite her attempts to hide it. Then my mother fell silent and I thought she had fallen asleep.

In the morning, she was still there looking at the roof of the tent with her eyes wide open. I greeted her good morning but she did not answer. I ran to Sidi Rajab. He was there walking behind the death cart and I called him.

"Help me, Sidi Rajab, my mother's not moving or talking to me," I said. Sidi Rajab threw his pickaxe and shovel to the ground and ran to me. The soldiers were screaming at him to get back but he did not care. Once we got to the tent, Sidi Rajab went down on his knees. He put his hand on Mum's neck and then held her wrist. Sidi Rajab touched her forehead and after that he closed her eyes.

"We belong to the Lord and to the Lord we shall return," Sidi Rajab said. Once I heard those words I knew my mother had passed away. I hugged Mum and in between the tears, I told her that I still needed her. Sidi Rajab took me into his arms.

"May the Lord bless her soul and receive her well." He patted my back and rubbed it up and down. I went outside and screamed, "Murderers!" The whole camp heard me. My mother was murdered. The black soldiers came and Sidi Rajab asked them to wheel the cart to here. Sidi Rajab carried her in his arms and put her gently on the cart. There were other bodies there too. I walked behind the cart and walked tall. The whole camp was walking behind me. Not one soldier said a thing. I escorted my mother all the way to the gate. I stood there until the cart disappeared into the horizon. Mum's words became a creed to me.

"Stay alive. We shall stay alive. We must get busy living. We shall not sit there and die."

* * *

Even in March, the second month of spring – the season that all Cyrenacians cherish the most – Al-agaila was still a horrid place to be in. The migrating small birds found a place to rest for a few days before continuing on their journey. Their singing had brought us something cheerful. Ten days ago, Sidi Rajab and I led a demonstration all the way to the bunkhouse. We demanded an end to the crimes against the women and threatened them that we would declare a hunger strike if they did not stop. We were quite prepared to die if it meant that our fellow Libyans would receive some ounce of respect. Nuri was released few days earlier and his family were cleared of any wrongdoing, but at the cost of losing twenty members of his family. Sidi Rajab gave him a letter to hand it to Libyan officials, hoping that it would find its way to someone in the Italian government in Benghazi to stop these dastardly crimes. I promised myself that I would strive to find the whereabouts of Aisha or learn what exactly happened to her that night.

I wandered for days on my own and spent many nights in our tent alone. I stayed with Sidi Rajab and Amina when I needed someone around me, but an unusual incident had occurred only two weeks after Nuri had left the camp and brought a sense of relief to everyone. The sleazy womanizer, Colonel Brachi, and all the soldiers who came shortly before Christmas, had been replaced from the camp and a new crew were deployed. Mergigo and a few others remained. Even Sidi Rajab himself did not know if the letter that they sent with Nuri was the reason or that the news of the crimes had been leaked to the governor. Whatever the reason, the weeping and screaming stopped and mothers no longer wandered around the camp looking for their missing daughters. A new colonel was in charge now and his name was Colonel Rossi, a very tall and stern looking man. Everyone showed respect when he was around. Everyone seemed to know my story as the new soldiers showed some sympathy toward me. I thought of everything my mother said to me. I ran to Sidi Rajab and asked him while catching my breath,

"Sidi Rajab, remember months ago you asked my mother if we could get me to do something that will help the sick and the weak and also Sidi Omar's men?"

"Yes, son, I remember very well. Why?" Sid Rajab asked.

"Well, I'm ready now," I confirmed.

"Are you sure, Salem, you want to do this?"

"Yes I'm ready. I'm doing it for the people of Al-agaila. I'm doing it for Aisha and Mum."

"Very well. I will not put you in any danger. I will keep a close eye on you and you will be fine, Salem. You are a clever boy." He then explained everything to me. "We need to get into the storerooms, Salem, and you are the only one who can do it."

At that stage, I had a fair grasp of the Italian language and some Italian soldiers showed a bit of sympathy toward me so I thought that I could do the job that Sidi Rajab asked of me.

"But how are we going to do that, Sidi Rajab?" I enquired.

"Well, it's a small idea. It came to me five months ago, but it could be very effective and it will bring us some sort of help."

"What is it, Sidi Rajab?"

"All right, you will be a shoeshine boy, Salem," Sidi Rajab revealed.

"A shoeshine boy? Could you tell me a bit more about it?"

"Yes, Salem. I will make you a shoeshine box and you will go to the soldiers and ask them if they want their boots to be shined. They might laugh at you first but eventually they will feel sorry for you and let you do it. That will bring you into the canteen and the bunkhouse. Your job is to find your way into the storerooms. Once there, you can get anything that will be useful to us. We'll make the box big enough to carry things inside it and the cover will be where you keep your rugs," Sidi Rajab explained.

"Will you train me, Sidi Rajab?"

"Yes, Salem, I will, but be warned: you might get a bit of stick from the boys and maybe others," Sidi Rajab said and continued, "but remember you're doing something great for everyone in the camp."

"I wouldn't let that intimidate me. No one will know anything of our plan and I won't let you down." I proudly accepted my role.

"You will be just fine. I know you will." Sid Rajab ruffled my hair while giving me a fatherly smile.

Three days later, I walked toward the bunkhouse carrying my shoeshine box strapped around my neck. I admit that I did not look the part of a shoeshine boy. My boots were two sizes too big and without laces. My Jalabiya was so dirty now that

I forgot what colour it was and my hair was so long, curly and greasy. I looked terrible, but that was how everybody looked in Al-agaila.

"*Signore, le scarpe sono polverosi posso brillare per te*," I said to one soldier informing him that his shoes were dusty and that I could shine them.

The soldier erupted in laughter and shouted to his friends, "Look everybody, we have a clown here."

"*Quanto si fanno pagare?*" shouted another, wanting to know the cost of my service.

"Signore, I don't charge money. I will take anything you can give," I said.

"Like what?" another asked.

"*Frutti, biscotti, al cioccolato*," I answered.

"You're a clown!" the same soldier retorted.

"Leave him alone," said the soldier who had enquired about the cost of my service. "This kid has been through a lot. As a matter of fact, I'll give him his first job. I like his way of thinking. He's a clever boy." He asked for my name and I found out that his name was Marco. "Come back to me in half an hour. I'll be in the canteen."

"*Grazie, signore*," I said before leaving. Marco was kind to me and through him I got to the canteen and got to know most of the soldiers by name. I observed all the doors and learned which door led to the storerooms and the one that led to the back of the canteen.

After my first job, Marco gave me a can of shoe dye and a shoe brush. I was giving Sidi Rajab daily reports about everything. I told him that I was ready and just waiting for the right moment. The canteen was big enough with lots of tables and chairs. There was a full kitchen and a long counter where the soldiers got served. It was so busy during lunch and dinner, but after the main meals, everyone went to the bunkhouse to get some rest. I came to the conclusion that after lunch is the best time to do it.

Within a week, I had earned everyone's trust and no one cared much about my movements, even when the mercenary soldiers tried sometimes to push me away. I told them that Officer Marco had given me permission and that kept them off my back, but Mergigo was always suspicious of me and normally raised one eyebrow.

"If I find out that you're telling a lie, I'll smash that box over your head," he always warned. Fortunately for me he never did. I started shining the soldiers' boots and getting lots of different things such as fresh bread, fruit, chocolate and even boiled eggs. I always ran back to Sidi Rajab and waited for him to return at sunset. Sidi Rajab was so proud of me, and as a reward he always gave me chocolate and other sweets, but his health began to deteriorate rapidly. He was coughing all the time, especially at night time. Despite his illness, Sidi Rajab always picked himself up and continued to do what he always did best which was helping people.

For me the moment of truth came one afternoon when I walked into the canteen. There were no soldiers present except for one Areterian mercenary who was sitting by the door to the storeroom, but he seemed to be having a nap with his head resting on his shoulder.

I have to do it, I thought, I won't get a better chance than this. I tiptoed around him and my heart pounded rampantly with every step I took closer to the door. My eyes were focused on him in case he discovered my presence. Once I got to the door, I hesitated for a minute and could not turn the handle. Quickly quelling the fears inside of me, I started turning the knob while retaining a close eye on the soldier. To my relief, the door was not locked and I pushed it open. I walked in and closed it behind me.

"Wow," I said silently and was awestruck by the sheer amount of food in the storeroom. There was enough to feed the whole camp. They were really heartless people. I wasted no time and put my box on the ground and then put in it everything that I could carry. Then I saw another door in the rear of the room and thought that since I am here now, I have to see what was behind that door. I opened it and it led to a decent sized yard. Windows were on two sides of the bunkhouse and the other side was a large room with a big door. There were a few doors leading to the bunkhouse from the yard. I made my way to that door using all the stealth of a commando. There was a big latch on it but with no locks so I pulled it very slowly. The door was stiff but after a minute, I managed to open it.

Inside it was not very dark as the room had few windows on the opposite side of the wall. There were guns displayed standing on racks. There were wooden boxes everywhere stacked on top of each other. Some of them were opened and I just took the lid off and there it was, shining like gold and the size of my finger, those deadly bullets – the same ones that took the life of my grandfather. I took two fistfuls and left, closing the door behind me. Having returned to the storeroom, I put the bullets in the box and secured the cover on top. I had a little difficulty in lifting it but once it was strapped around my neck, the box became easier to carry. I opened the door a fraction to see if the guard was still asleep and he was. I opened it enough to get myself through.

My heart pounded furiously the whole time. I was sweating but kept my nerve. Once I made it to the outside of the canteen, I sighed and calmed myself, then walked toward our tent as it was closer to walk to. I covered the shine box with the cloak and then I went to see the children to kill some time until the return of Sidi Rajab from his daily work.

Once the sun began to hide behind the horizon to mark the end of another working day, men returned from the work outside the camp. Sidi Rajab was there, but he looked so tired and he was losing weight rapidly. His cough was getting worse. I did not want to risk taking the box to his tent, so I waited until we got to the queue for dinner. There I told him that I had something to show him. The three of us went back to my tent. I moved the cloak before opening the box. Sidi Rajab and Amina were astounded by what they saw.

"Oh, Lord, Salem, you're an amazing boy! You're a hero like your father. I am so proud of you," Sidi Rajab said while holding me in a tight embrace, showing his appreciation and support.

"God bless you, son. This is truly the work of a brave man. You're an exceptional boy," Amina said.

Sidi Rajab held some bullets in his hand and said, "Sidi Omar's men will be very happy to see them. They are desperate for ammunition and food. You did really great, Salem." Sidi Rajab could not believe the kind of food they ate when they deprived us of the very basic necessities. "Salem, my son, I want you to come with us tonight to meet some people. I want you to know everything. You're part of the struggle and you must be there with us."

That night Sidi Rajab took me to a tent in the very far side of the camp. There were some men and women sitting there in a circle. The minute we entered the tent, all stood up as a mark of respect for Sidi Rajab and his wife. I brought the shoeshine box with me. It was cumbersome, but this was the only way, otherwise it would draw unwanted attention from the guards. Some of the men present were unsure why a young boy of my age should be there when adults were discussing things of a sensitive nature. Some of them could not hide their feelings on the matter and it showed on their faces. But that all changed when Sidi Rajab asked me to put the box down and then he opened it. Their jaws dropped and everyone was astonished by what they saw. Then Sidi Rajab introduced me to the men and women as, "Salem the Brave". They all heard of my name before. Once Sidi Rajab mentioned my name and told them of what I had been doing, they all shook hands with me and started praising me. That night Sidi Rajab told them about me in great detail and what I could contribute to the camp and the men outside.

As night time approached, Sidi Rajab spoke as if he knew his time on Earth was coming to an end. He told them that he wanted me to be part of the meetings and he appointed his wife as the link. On the same night, something very exciting occurred. I had to go to the barbwire with Sidi Rajab and another two men to meet some of Sidi Omar's soldiers and gave them the provisions we had collected for the week and received news from their end. We snuck out, avoiding the guards and the spotlight on the tower. It felt so great, but I must say that deep down, I knew Sidi Rajab was going to meet them for the last time. His cough grew worse and he told them that he might die.

My secret visits to the storeroom and ammunitions' room continued and I even started to gain access to the bunkhouse. The children sometimes followed and threw stones at me, calling me names. Some of the names were very harsh like "traitor", but I always walked tall with a big smile, reminding myself that they did not know what I was really doing.

Two days later, Sidi Rajab collapsed while walking behind the cart. The soldiers were shouting at him to stand up. They even lashed him with the whip, but Sidi Rajab was too weak and too ill to stand. He was carried by two men to his tent. Amina and I took turns in looking after him.

One afternoon at the end of April, a beautiful civilian car arrived and parked outside the bunkhouse. Few soldiers rushed to receive the car and one of them opened the driver's door. An attractive Italian lady exited the vehicle and then the back door was opened and two children around my age emerged. There was a boy and a girl, both smartly dressed. I stood not far from where the girl was and she regarded me for a few seconds and smiled. I felt like I knew her and it was a strange feeling.

I was carrying my shine box. Many women and children came closer to see them. Everyone hoped that they might bring about a positive change. Then the colonel came out from his office.

"You made it, darling!" he shouted while running toward her. He kissed her and then he ran toward the children and embraced them.

"We missed you, papa," both children said while in his arms. I must say that those moments touched my heart and I pictured myself with Mum and Dad. I truly missed them. The colonel took his family to his office. His wife turned her head toward where I was standing, but I had moved from that spot as one soldier asked me to move back. That day I did not make any attempt to go inside the canteen. I sat on the steps of the bunkhouse and within an hour, the Rossi children came out.

"*Buongiorno, qual ê il tuo nome?*" the girl asked.

"Salem," I answered. She was so cute and wore a white dress with white shoes.

"What is this box you're wearing around your neck?" she asked and I could tell that she was quite curious.

"It's my shine box. I shine soldiers' boots for food. I don't take money. It's no good to me here."

"Why do you look like you haven't washed or changed your clothes in a long time?" she pressed further.

"I have no other clothes and we've no water to wash ourselves. I mean they don't let us wash ourselves," I replied and then the boy got closer.

"This is a strange place. Why are all these tents behind the barbwire and why does everyone look so miserable?" the boy enquired.

"I don't know why, but I think they're punishing us for something we didn't do," I informed him.

"I'll ask my father later, but who do you live here with?" The girl put the question to me.

"I don't have a family of my own. I lost all my family." I was unable to withhold the sadness that dwelled in my heart.

"You poor thing," the girl said.

"What's your name?" I enquired.

"My name is Sofia and this is my brother Alexander."

At that moment, the colonel and his wife came out.

"Don't get too close to him. You might catch lice off him," the colonel shouted.

"Do you really have lice?" Sofia asked.

"*Si*, I have lots of it. Do you have lice yourself?"

Sofia and Alexander laughed at my innocence. The lady was smiling and she came down the steps. Once she reached the bottom step, Rossi's wife looked deep into my eyes.

"You have very beautiful but sad eyes. What's your name?"

"My name is Salem."

"My name is Allegra, Allegra Rossi. I am Sofia and Alexander's mother and this is my husband," the lady replied. "Come on, kids, say goodbye to Salem. We must go inside to seek some rest after the long journey." She looked into my eyes again and smiled, then turned holding the children in her arms.

I ran back to Sidi Rajab, who was in his sickbed. I gave him a sip of water and Amina was taking a nap beside him. Afterwards, I told him about the people that I had just met.

"Everybody loves Salem. You're a special boy," Sidi Rajab said while putting his hand on his mouth, alerting me that he was about to cough.

The next day I went to the bunkhouse and Sofia and Alexander were there. As I approached them, Mergigo the Areterian came charging to shoo me away. Sofia, however, ordered him to back off and informed him that I was their friend. Secretly I relished this moment because Mergigo felt so small, but he raised that eyebrow again and bore an expression that said, "I'll get you later". The Rossi children revealed that they were here for the weekend and would be leaving early Monday morning, returning again every two weeks until their father finished in a month's time. They asked me to sit with them on the steps of the bunkhouse and tell them everything about myself and the camp. I told them so many stories about the Green Mountain and my dog, Saiyad. I also explained how I lost my family and about my close relationship with Sidi Rajab and his wife, Amina. Sofia and Alexander listened to my tales with great interest. I saw tears in Sofia's eyes. Signora Rossi was standing by the door looking at the three of us with a big smile on her kind face. It was time for me to go and I said goodbye.

"I won't be able to see you in the morning because I have to look after Sidi Rajab, but I can't wait to see you in two weeks time."

Sidi Rajab's health was worsening by the minute and soon he coughed up blood. A constant stream of visitors were coming and going all day. After everyone had left, he asked me to come closer to him and he held my hand.

"Salem, my son, I don't think I have much time left here in this world. I want to tell you that I am so lucky to have met you and always remember that life is full of surprises and you have seen the worst of them. There is nothing that can break you. You can only rise, shine and be strong. I'll miss you."

"I'll miss you, too. If you meet my family in Heaven, will you tell them that I miss them a lot?"

He smiled and nodded his head. "Come a bit closer to me, Salem." Sidi Rajab hugged me and kissed my forehead. I knew that he was saying goodbye and this would be the last time I would feel his embrace in this life. He asked for some time alone with his wife. I kissed his hand, and when I went outside the tent, I broke down and cried. While outside the tent, I remembered his words to me that in death, sometimes it is freedom for the suffering souls. I guess Sidi Rajab wanted to be free.

Amina's weeping brought me back into the tent. She looked at me with a face full of sorrow and said that Rajab submitted his soul to the Lord. "May Allah substitute your loss with patience," she prayed.

News of his passing quickly spread and everyone inside the camp felt the loss too. The death cart stopped outside the tent and two soldiers came and lifted him without any respect and then threw him in the cart. I walked behind it for the whole day. More bodies were taken from different tents. I walked behind the cart all the way to the gates because the man who buried thousands of bodies was now going to be buried and without a funeral. I felt alone in the camp.

Signora Rossi made two trips to Al-agaila. The last time they came, they took Signore Rossi with them. She told me that she would get me out of this horrible place.

As I returned to Amina to check on her, the wind started howling like a hungry pack of wolves and I knew a storm was brewing, adding further misery to this hellhole.

CHAPTER TWELVE

June was a scorching month. I remember sitting on the steps of the bunkhouse, seeking shelter from the sun. The boots Bubaker gave me became worn with holes appearing on the sole. In addition, I picked up the lice from my neck and the side of my face as they escaped from the tangled, greasy hair. I was always ready for them by placing them on the steps and crushing them with my boots.

Things were very quiet and the people did not care much about the soldiers, as death became their daily wish. After one year in Al-agaila, you prayed for the Grim Reaper to pay you a visit. In the Camp of the Suffering, people actually envied the dead, and when they heard that someone had passed away, they actually praised the deceased for leaving this hellish domain.

A car arrived at the camp again. Soldiers started coming out of the bunkhouse and people exited their tents. Even the Areterians who were sleeping in the shade of the walls of the bunkhouses, woke very quickly. For the prisoners of Al-agaila it was a glimpse of hope every time a car came. To them it might have some news of their release. The car started taking shape as it got closer and was a shiny sleek black car.

As it reached the checkpoint at the gates, the vehicle halted while the soldier was engaged in a conversation with the driver. An order was given for the bar to be raised and it moved toward the bunkhouses and to the new colonel's office. When it stopped, two Areterians hurried to the car and opened the doors. Two beautiful, elegant ladies emerged. Colonel Delveccio came out to investigate the unusual commotion outside his office. I recognised the driver. She was the alluring Signora Rossi. She wore a light blue dress with a hat to match it and white fancy shoes. Rossi's wife was accompanied by another tall lady wearing white dress and red hat and red shoes. Everybody was stunned by their beauty and elegance.

"*Buongiorno, grazie mille,*" Signora Rossi said.

"*Molte grazie*," the other lady spoke at the same time to the African soldiers.

Colonel Delveccio took his cap off and descended the steps to greet them. "*Buongiorno, Signora Rossi*," he said while shaking her hand. "How was your trip?"

"Long and tiring," she replied and then pointed to her friend. "This is my good friend, Signora Rossellini."

"*Piacere di conoscerti*," the colonel greeted while kissing Signora Rossellini on the cheek. Signora Rossi promised me once that she would take me out of this place someday and I wondered if that was the reason for her visit. Signora Rossellini noticed that all the Italian soldiers had come out of their bunkhouses to look at them and she could not resist the temptation of flirting by smiling at them to acknowledge the attention.

"Come with me, ladies, to the canteen. You are very welcome and you will stay with us for food and fresh drinks before we conduct the business that brought you here," the colonel said while showing them the way.

Signora Rossi noticed me and shouted while waving, "*Buongiorno*, Salem. I'll see you later." I smiled.

Everybody looked at me with faces full of disbelief. I felt shy and just smiled at her. Then the officers and soldiers returned to their posts. The Areterians hollered at the women and children to go back to their tents.

I sat on the steps and put my boots on. Two Areterians came and sat not far from me. They took their funny fezzes off and started speaking in their own language. Neither of them said a word to me since everybody knew the hell that I had been through. I also had formed some sort of friendship with them and they knew that I no longer feared them. I tightened the boots and went straight to the tent that I shared now with Sidi Hamed and his wife, Kadega since the departure of Sidi Rajab's and his wife from this world.

Couple of hours later an Italian soldier came. "Salem, Salem. Are you there?"

"*Si, Signore Bruno*," I yelled back.

"Hurry. The colonel wants you."

I came out quickly and followed him.

"You're some lucky kid, Salem. We will miss you here," Marco said.

"Why, Signore Marino? Do you think I will be leaving here?" I had a big grin on my face.

"You will find out for yourself. Say nothing," Marco instructed.

As soon as we got there, Signora Rossi and Signora Rossellini were sitting at a big table in the canteen accompanied by Colonel Delveccio and some other officers. Signora Rossi stood and came toward me and kissed me on the cheek.

"I'm sorry I didn't come earlier," Signora Rossi said.

"*Grazie, Signora* Rossi," I replied, smiling.

Then Signora Rossellini looked at me and said, "You're a beautiful boy." No one could believe what was happening. Even the officers were making some remarks and asking her from time to time if she was sure about what she was doing.

"Well then, we must carry on, Signora Rossi. Marco, go and get the shaving machine and give him a hair cut," the colonel ordered.

"Si, Signore," Marco replied.

Some minutes later we were in one of the bunkhouse rooms. Marco sat me on the chair and then he turned to Signora Rossi.

"How much hair am I to cut off?" Marco asked.

"All of it," Signora Rossi answered. Marco's machine took a big chunk of my hair.

Within minutes, I was bald and it felt so good. Sidi Rajab always told me that Signora Rossi would come to take me away from here and he always said that I deserved a better life.

"That's fine. It suits you, Salem," Signora Rossi commented.

"Si, you look even more handsome than earlier," Signora Rossellini added. Then the colonel ordered some soldiers to give Signora Rossi's car a check before their departure and he turned his attention to me.

"Go now, Salem and get ready to leave this place with the ladies," he said. "You know that you are the luckiest boy in this camp, you are not just leaving this place but with the most beautiful women I have ever seen."

The ladies smiled acknowledging the compliment.

"Grazie, signore," I replied while turning to run toward the door.

When I got outside, there was a huge group of the camp members waiting for me.

"Skin head!" a boy shouted. Yousef put his hand on my head and remarked that it was like a watermelon.

"No, it's like the back of an old worm," another piped up. They all erupted in laughter. Then Sidi Hamed stepped out from the crowd and took me by the hand. We went straight to his tent and there was his wife and a few women who knew my mother. Then the children came in and gathered around me and Sidi Hamed.

"Listen very carefully, Salem." Then he took something out of a bucket and said it was for me. "It's a silver chain Sidi Rajab gave to me before his death to hand it to you when the time was right." It was a beautiful chain with a verse from the Quran engraved on it. "It's yours. Your mother gave it to Sidi Rajab when she felt that she might not make it. It's from your father, you must keep it safe. Your mother didn't want to give it to you in fear that maybe the soldiers would take it from you."

Then I remembered that dawn when my father left us and when he gave something to Mum and leaned on her shoulder to whisper something.

"Thank you, Sidi Hamed. I'll keep it and protect it for as long as I live," I replied with a nod of gratitude. I put it around my neck. "I have to get my things."

They all laughed and Sidi Hamed said, "You have nothing except that pair of battered shoes and your patched Jalabiya. They even took your hair. You're lucky to get out alive," Sidi Hamed drove home the point that had already been made clear to me several times that day. Before the goodbyes, Sidi Hamed held my hand and said, "You must be grateful and patient. God is definitely watching over you and don't forget to pray for us.

You know that we will pray for you, now stand up and say farewell to the 'Camp of Suffering'."

Everyone became teary–eyed. I hugged them all while saying farewell and knew that I would never see them again. It was the hardest thing for me to do. Even though I was gaining my freedom, part of me wished to stay here. Somehow, I felt that I was betraying them by leaving.

"Go now, Salem, and never look back. You have nothing here," Sidi Hamed advised and at that moment, Mehrawi, an Areterian soldier came.

"Come on, the ladies are waiting for you and you are here yapping away, you little devil!" he yelled.

"I was gathering my things," I said.

"Things? What things? You have nothing but fleas in this place," he reminded me while raising his stick up in the air. Everybody laughed. It was good to see the prisoners of Al-agaila retaining the natural Bedouin sense of humour. I walked slowly and everybody followed me. When I got to our tent that I shared with Mum and Aisha, I stopped and then turned toward it. I could feel many eyes on me and Mehrawi did not say a word.

I entered the empty tent and somehow I could smell Mum and Aisha. Tears sauntered down my cheek as I fondly remembered Aisha's girly giggle when she was amused and Mum warning me not to go far.

"Goodbye," I said. "You will always be in my heart." I wiped the tears from my face with the back of my hand before marching toward Signora Rossi's car.

"Well, give my best regards to Signore Rossi. Drive safely. *Arrivederci, buona fortuna*," the colonel said while kissing the ladies farewell. Signora Rossi opened the back door for me.

"*Entrare*. Don't be afraid, Salem," Signora Rossi said in a very soft voice. I felt safe and looked at the people of Al-agaila for the last time. With tears still falling, I smiled at them and sat in.

"We inspected the car and we put in the back some reserve fuel and water in case you need it," one of the soldiers informed Signora Rossi.

"Grazie mille. Arrivederci," Signora Rossi replied and then the ladies got into the car. The engine was running and we moved off. It was my first time in a car and what a car it was!

As we approached the gates, the crowd marched after the vehicle and everybody was shouting, "marbouha, marbouha" wishing me "good luck." The gates opened and soldiers saluted the ladies. When we exited the camp, a voice inside me proudly proclaimed, "I am free, I am free!"

The farther we drove, the more Al-agaila gradually disappeared. It was only later that I felt the enormous size of the tragedy and its impact on those who survived the concentration camps. A plethora of harrowing memories such as my farewell to Dad, the march to the hill, my grandfather's death, my friends, Bubaker and Sidi Rajab, the snatching of Aisha and her screaming amongst other memories all passed through my mind like a slideshow. It was only later in life that I learned the true pain that Graziani and Mussolini had inflicted upon the Libyan people. These images will remain with me for the rest of my life, but I learnt a lot from my father, mother, Aisha, my grandfather, Bubaker and Sidi Rajab. My family taught me to let go and to cope not through hate and anger, but with love and compassion. I learned that those who got hurt should not retaliate and do the same to others. Al-agaila, Slooq, Al-magroon, Al-brega and the other concentration camps were nothing but a stark reminder of how cruel mankind can be.

I kept looking until the Camp of Suffering had completely disappeared and was now nothing but a dot in the horizon.

When I turned around, Signora Rossi turned her head gently and said, "You're free now." Her face was glowing and she had a fabulous smile. Tiredness overcame me as my frail body sunk into the comfortable leather interior. I slipped into a dream, not knowing what lay ahead.

CHAPTER THIRTEEN

I must have slept for quite a while because when I woke up, it was dark. The cranking and chirping noise the engine was making before it came to a stop and the gentle calling of Signora Rossi had disturbed me from my slumber. It took me about ten seconds or so to realise where I was as I thought it was a dream.

"*Buonasera*," Signora Rossi said while I was stretching my hands and wiping my eyes.

No, this was not a dream, I thought, and I am definitely with two ladies and away from that hellhole.

"*Buonasera*," I replied with a wide smile. Signora Rossellini greeted me also. We were outside a building, but I did not know what it was.

"It's a hotel," Signora Rossi said.

" We're staying in the Roma Hotel for the night," Signora Rossellini added.

"Where are we?" I asked.

"We are in Ajdabiya. It's a small city a few hundred kilometres from the city of Benghazi," Signora Rossi explained. I did not have a clue where Ajdabiya was, never mind Benghazi. As we got out of the car, the air was cool and refreshing, especially after a hot day in Al-agaila. Soon the ladies opened the car boot and took out couple of small suitcases and a sack.

"Let me please give you a hand," I insisted.

"*Grazie*," Signora Rossi answered and handed me the small sack. The hotel looked nice and neat. We took a few steps toward the entrance and then we were greeted by the proprietor of the hotel.

"Buonasera, Signora siete I Benevento," a woman greeted the ladies. Once she saw me, she shouted, "Go away you little Arab beggar!"

"He's with us," Signora Rossi responded. The lady immediately changed her attitude toward me and smiled.

"*Scusa la mia ignoranza e la signora, mia perdoni*," she said.

"Don't worry, we all can make mistakes when it comes to that," Signora Rossi responded.

We walked into the reception and it was very warm and welcoming and had extremely comfortable seats. There were tables and dim lights came from the lamps fitted on the walls. There were lots of paintings and mirrors on the walls. I noticed that many army personnel were present there also. Some of them were dining and others were drinking, but the moment we stood in the middle of the reception area, everybody stopped and looked at us with a cold, hard stare. The reason was very obvious: it was a mixture of two beautiful Italian women and a filthy Arab boy.

"What can I do for you, ladies?" the receptionist asked.

"Si, one dubble bed room please?" Signora Rossi responded very quickly.

"We have rather large and luxurious room. It's yours. Anything else?"

"Si, could you arrange a hot bath in the room while we dine?" Signora Rossi asked.

"Si, signora, it will be ready when you are." Few minutes later she led the way to a table. "Here you are." She handed Signora Rossi the key and continued, "The menus are on the way."

"Grazie mille," the ladies replied. As we sat down, Signora Rossellini took a cigarette from a fancy case and before she lit the cigarette, she started with lighting the small candle in the middle of the table.

"I would like to go to the toilet," I asked politely.

"Si, come with me."

I followed Signora Rossi when she requested directions to the toilets. The receptionist pointed to them.

"There you go, Salem, this is yours, and when you're finished, wait outside the door for me. I need to go to the ladies myself."

It was something I had never seen. It was so clean with mirrors and washbasins with lots of soaps and towels. After relieving myself, I washed my hands, but it seemed like an endless job.

Once I got out, Signora Rossi led the way once again to our table.

The landlady had just returned to our table with a small notebook and a pen. "Well, the special today is minestrone soup followed by roasted chicken with vegetables."

"That sounds good to me. I'll have that," Signora Rossi said.

"I think we'll all have that. *Grazie*, and can we have a bottle of red wine and a glass of milk for little Salem here?" Signora Rossellini added.

Soon the lady arrived with the drinks and poured a little measure into Signora Rossi's glass. Signora Rossi smelled the wine while swivelling the glass before taking a sip. She paused for a second and then she said, "It's fine.".

The landlady then poured another good measure in both glasses and put the bottle on the table. "Enjoy," she said.

"*Grazie*," Signora Rossi replied.

Signora Rossi and Rossellini chatted away while I sipped slowly from my hot glass of milk. Officers were constantly eyeing the ladies. It was not long before the soups arrived along with a basket of homemade bread.

"This is real soup," "What we used to get in Al-agaila was hot water."

"You will eat real food, Salem, from now on. I promise you," Signora Rossi vowed.

"Do you know, Salem, that Signora Rossi wanted to take you from that horrible place from the moment she saw you, and she fought very hard in order to do that," Signora Rossellini revealed.

"Thank you, Signora Rossi, for taking me out of there. I'll never forget that," I replied.

The main course was served and I was in a dilemma, as I did not know how to use the fork and knife, as it was not custom of ours..

"Eat, Salem, the way you feel comfortable with," Signora Rossi instructed, putting me at ease.

As we used to say in the Green Mountain, "You don't teach an orphan how to cry". The roasted chicken was soon devoured.

The ladies looked at me with sympathetic faces. They knew that in Al-agaila we were subjected to sinister and systematic starvation. Now everyone seemed to be keen on us and those officers were still looking at the ladies, hoping that they would get some sort of acknowledgment for their efforts. Looking back on it now, I can understand why the soldiers were unable to lure their eyes away from Signora Rossi and Rossellini; they were amazing looking women.

The ladies continued to chat amongst themselves while I was enjoying the dessert that Signora Rossi ordered for me. It was some sort of pie with cream.

"Is everything okay with your husband, and how do you think he's going to react?" Signora Rossellini asked while taking a drag of her cigarette.

"Well, I must say that he worked very hard in order to get the papers right and he put in some good arguments as I instructed him, but it wasn't easy. He was always reluctant to the idea," Signora Rossi answered.

"Do you think that he'll agree to let you take him in to live with you in the house?"

"I have to be very careful in how to approach that. You know he's a very stubborn man," Signora Rossi explained while sighing.

"I don't think it will be easy knowing his stubbornness. Everything he did was out of love for you, you know what I mean?"

I knew that the ladies were talking in a coded fashion so that I would not fully understand what they were saying.

"He's a military man, at the end of the day and his loyalty is to Il Duce and the King. He doesn't realise the pain and suffering we have inflicted upon the natives," Signora Rossi spoke in an annoyed tone.

"Lower your voice, my dear. The place is full of officers. Let's change the subject and have some fun," Signora Rossellini said while turning her head toward the table on her right with a flirtatious smile. The two officers smiled in return and raised their glasses to toast the ladies' presence. Both women laughed and raised their glasses. The officers seized the opportunity as one of them approached our table, putting one hand on it and leaning in closely to Signora Rossellini.

"*Buonasera*," the officer greeted.

"*Buonasera*," the ladies replied.

"My colleague and I would like to invite you to have a drink with us. Forgive me for not introducing myself first as it's very seldom for an army man to come across an elegant and beautiful woman but to come across two in one day is surely a once in a lifetime event."

The ladies blushed, exchanging eye contact and acknowledging his charm.

"I am Roberto, Capitano Roberto Colombo, and my friend is," He threw a thumb in his comrade's direction, "Colonel Frank De Niro."

"*Si, grazie*. My name is Angelica Rossellini and this is my good friend, Allegra Rossi and this is our young companion, Salem. We'll take your charming invitation onboard. We just have to take care of some business and freshen up so we might see you later," Signora Rossellini answered politely.

"I take it you're staying for the night?" the captain asked.

"Si, we are and we will be heading to Benghazi in the morning," Signora Rossi replied.

"We are heading to Mesrata in the morning, too. We are here since yesterday," the officer added.

"Well, nice meeting you," Signora Rossi ended the conversation.

"*Buonasera*, have a good evening," Captain Colombo said. "Please join us later.". He returned to his table. Both women seemed so charmed that they started giggling. The landlady arrived at our table.

"The bath and room are ready when you are," she said and then gestured with a nod of her head to the two officers. "Those men have paid your bill. They're very generous and have sent you this bottle of wine."

"Grazie mille. We will take it with us to the room. Come on, Salem. We'll retire to our room. You have to get your bath and a goodnight's sleep," Signora Rossi said while raising the bottle in the air.

Signora Rossellini said goodbye to the officers. "*Arrivederci.*"

It was not long before Signora Rossi was pushing in the door of room number ten. She threw her handbag on the bed.

"It's not bad at all. I'll fix couple of glasses before we bath Salem," Signora Rossi said.

"Good idea," Signora Rossellini replied. "I think the Capitano was a very handsome and charming man. Don't you agree?"

"I agree with you," Signora Rossi answered while putting her suitcase on the bed. She opened it and took out some items. "Salem, I want you to go to the bath. Take your clothes off and place them in this bag. We'll get rid of them forever once you do that. Get yourself in the bath. We will come to you when you're ready," Signora Rossi instructed.

It was a very clean and luxurious bathroom. The floor was tiled with white marble and half the walls were covered with small tiles to match the floor. The bath itself was in the middle of the room and was covered in lots of foam. Steam rose up from it. Again, this was something that I had never laid eyes on before. I took off my shoes and my Bedouin clothes and placed them in a bag as Signora Rossi instructed and cautiously slipped into the bath as the water was very hot. Soon my body became accustomed to it and I was sitting in the middle, totally covered in a mountain of scented white foam. It is hard to describe what I felt. In Al-agaila we were deprived of everything. I did not wash myself for the whole year.

I shouted, telling the ladies that I was ready. Seconds later the two ladies entered the bathroom holding a glass of wine each and some bag with stuff in it.

"Salem, you will feel like you're a new person when we're finished with you," Signora Rossi said.

"What do you think of the place?" Signora Rossellini asked me while pouring more scented oil into the bath.

"It is a million times better than Al-agaila," I answered.

"Anything is better than Al-agaila, even the dog-houses and the pig sties," Signora Rossellini added.

"Let's not waste any time. We'll need a lot of it to do the job right," Signora Rossi said.

Signora Rossellini started with my back with a sponge while Signora Rossi was lifting my feet and started scraping them. The feeling was indescribable and no one would ever believe that this was happening to a Bedouin boy who was a few hours earlier, a prisoner in a concentration camp. I started feeling my body once again. I felt human. Signora Rossellini took some foam and put it on my nose.

"*Pagliaccio poco*," Signora Rossellini laughed, calling me a little clown. Then Signora Rossi began sprinkling water on Signora Rossellini. I got a little excited and splashed the water with both my hands. We were laughing like three children and their dresses got wet. I could see the shape of their bodies. Signora Rossellini spotted me looking at her breasts. I felt shy and embarrassed. Signora Rossellini smiled and patted me on my head. Then out came the nail and toes clippers. It was like a dream. The ladies were sipping their wine from time to time and chatting away.

After at least two hours, Signora Rossi handed me a big towel and clean clothes. "It's pyjamas, Salem. Put them on when you finish drying yourself."

"*Grazie*, Signora Rossi. Grazie mille, Signora Rossellini," I said, bowing my head in appreciation. Few minutes later I was fully dressed and the pyjamas were a beautiful bright blue and so silky. If I am to be honest, that was probably the best bath I had in all my life.

"*Oh, mio Dio*, you are one handsome boy," Signora Rossi praised me, Signora Rossellini agreed with her and hugged me. Soon I was lying in the middle of the huge bed, feeling so good. My eyes started getting heavier. For the first time in a year, I went to bed feeling safe, content, clean and fed. Signora Rossi unplugged the bath and exclaimed in abhorrence at all the dirt that had been removed from my body. I smiled then fell into a deep sleep. To me, it felt that I slept a whole year in one night and when I opened my eyes in the early hours of the morning, I was sharing the bed with the most beautiful Italian ladies I had ever seen.

CHAPTER FOURTEEN

By the time Signora Rossi and Signora Rossellini were washing and getting ready, I was fully dressed and ready to go. I stood in front of the mirror and I must say that I did not recognise myself, but felt happy. Signora Rossi had brought me some new clothes to wear. A beautiful brown shirt, shoes, belt and black trousers.

"You are the same size as my son, Alexander, so they should fit you," Signora Rossi said. When the ladies came out of the bathroom, they could not believe that I was the same boy who was yesterday a prisoner in Al-agaila.

When we made our way toward the reception area, the place was full of people having their breakfast. No one looked at me as they did the previous night. As a matter of fact, the landlady did not recognise me at first and greeted me in a benevolent way. She even asked me if I had a good sleep.

"Yes, like a log," I told her. The ladies laughed and continued sorting out things. After a light breakfast, we were on our way to Benghazi. This time I did not sleep, but I was looking out the windows for the duration of our journey to the city.

"This is Jelyana," Signora Rossi announced. "It's a beautiful beach and we spend a lot of time here. I'll bring you sometime, along with the kids. We are at the outskirts of the city so it shouldn't be long now," Signora Rossellini informed me while looking at her face through a small mirror, putting some make-up on with a brush.

It was not long before the buildings began appearing and soon we were driving through beautiful streets with lots of modern buildings and shops. It was a vibrant place. The ladies were showing me and pointing at every shop and building and telling me something about them. I fell in love with the city from the very minute we entered it. My father told me about Benghazi when he visited the city with his father a long time ago and I still remember very well what he said about the place,

"Son, do you know that the people of the city call it, 'The Mother of the Orphans'." This was proven to be correct as the city took me into her arms and I would be her son forever.

"This is Paizzacane," Signora Rossi announced. "This is where we live. It's the Italian neighbourhood." It was very busy and many people walked on the streets.

Then Signora Rossellini turned her head very quickly and shouted, "Look, Salem, look! You see that place with tables outside it? It's Allegra's Café. Do you know something, Salem? You'll be working here. You will be giving Allegra a hand. I think you will be a great helper."

"I will be very happy. I'll do everything for Signora Rossi," I replied. Signora Rossi liked what she heard and this was expressed by her broad smile.

"He'll be great. He seems to be very loyal and mature for his age," Signora Rossellini commented. Fifteen minutes later, Signora Rossi was pointing at a tall building, saying that her apartment is on the second floor, but we had to go to the back street where the car park and the entrance were. Once the car stopped and the engine was switched off, Signora Rossi opened the door and started stretching and yawning at the same time. Then Signora Rossellini did the same before opening the door for me. It was sometime in the afternoon and the minute I got out of the car, I was hit by a cool breeze as we were so close to the sea. Signora Rossellini asked Signora Rossi to open the boot of the car to get her luggage, but before that, Signora Rossi insisted that she should come for refreshments before she went home.

"No, I better not. That grumpy old man of yours could be there and you know that he doesn't hide his feelings towards me." Signora Rossellini grabbed her bag and gave Signora Rossi a big hug. "I enjoyed every bit of the trip with you and you're truly a good friend." Then Signora Rossellini came to me and said, "Salem, I have heard a lot about you before and I really liked you before seeing you yesterday. Now I can tell you that we're going to be good friends." Then she leaned in and kissed me on the cheek. "*Arrivederci*," Signora Rossellini shouted. We watched her until she disappeared.

"She lives on the next street," Signora Rossi said and then she grabbed her own luggage before locking the car. "Salem, you know I had to fight hard to get you out of that nasty place and I must tell you that I put so much pressure on my husband to do it and because of his military rank and influence, we succeeded in getting permission to get you out of Al-agaila, but he doesn't know that I want you to live with us so I want you to listen to me very carefully. My husband's a very typical military man so if at any stage you feel like he is rude or ignorant, don't take it personally because he's like that with everyone. Do you understand?"

"*Si*, I understand."

"Come on, then. The children will be very delighted to see you, Salem."

I have to admit that I was not too eager to meet Signore Rossi and as I approached the entrance to the apartment building, the fear increased and weighed heavily on my heart. An African servant came forward and he greeted Signora Rossi in a humorous Italian accent.

"Please, signora, leave your bags to me. I will take them," he said while taking them off her.

We took the stairs to the second floor. Everything was floored with marble and then the servant put the luggage on the ground. Signora Rossi took something out of her handbag and handed it to him.

"*Grazie mille*, Signora Rossi," he said and made his way downstairs again. Signora Rossi organised herself before knocking at the door. She had her arm around my shoulder and wanted me to feel welcome. Almost immediately, the door opened and a middle-aged Italian lady greeted her very warmly.

"*Buongiorno*, Signora Rossi."

"*Si*, it's good to be back."

Seconds later, Sofia and Alexander ran out and embraced their mother. The children knew perfectly well that their mother had taken this trip especially to take me out from the concentration camp but to their surprise, I looked so different from the last time they saw me. Sofia and Alexander were amazed.

"This is unbelievable! It's hard to tell that it's you, Salem," Sofa said aghast. "We're pleased to see you."

"*Si*, you look like an Italian boy, Salem," Alexander said.

"*Grazie mille*," I replied full of excitement.

Signora Rossi gave a little laugh. It was such a beautiful place. The furniture was expensive looking and this was a whole new experience for me. There were huge bookshelves and leather sofas. Beautiful paintings hung on the walls. There were so many doors on each side. Then Signora Rossi opened a big door and music hit my ears. It was like something from my dreams and the smell of tobacco permeated my nostrils.

Signora Rossi and her children entered the room. I stood outside the door but I could still see what was happening inside. Signore Rossi was sitting on an armchair, puffing away on his pipe and sipping from a small glass. Once Signore Rossi spotted Allegra, he greeted her without moving from his chair.

"Buongiorno, how was your trip?" Signore Rossi asked while Signora Rossi was leaning down to kiss him.

"It was long and tiring, but we spent a beautiful night in the Hotel Roma in Ajdabiya." Then she turned and beckoned me to enter.

As I walked in, Signore Rossi scrutinised me as he did not believe what he was seeing, but then nodded his head and went back to smoking his pipe while gazing at the ceiling. I took it as a form of acknowledgement and some sort of greeting. Signora Rossi quickly responded by taking us to the kitchen for some refreshments. We all ran behind her to a big and very modern kitchen. We each grabbed a chair and sat down.

"By the way, Salem, do you think you'll go back there to that weird place? I mean are you going to miss it?" Sofia asked.

"Did you find time to play there and what sort of games did you play?" Alexander now asked.

Signora Rossi came to my rescue. "Don't burden him with all these questions. Give him time to relax after a long journey.

Salem is not going anywhere. Salem will stay with us for as long as it takes."

"But I don't mind the questions, Signora Rossi," I said, and told them about my miserable life in that Godforsaken place. The children listened intently as I told them stories about the soldiers' treatment to all the prisoners and how cruel they were to my family. Soon Signora Rossi and Signorina De Luca – the child minder – organised some drinks and cakes for us. They were delicious.

After we ate, Alexander said, "Come with me, Salem. I'll show you a great view from the rear balcony. You'll love it."

I looked at Signora Rossi to seek her permission and she nodded her head in approval. Sofia grabbed me by the hand and we ran after Alexander. Once we were in the big balcony, Alexander shouted, "Look, Salem, isn't that beautiful?"

"Yes, it is fabulous and the air is so fresh." The apartment overlooked the port and there were many ships docked at the harbour . Alexander pointed at a small crowd.

"Do you see that crowd, Salem?" he asked.

"Yes, who are they?"

"They're local fishermen and Italians selling their fresh fish. It's my favourite place. I just love fish and by the way, Salem, I'll take you fishing with me sometime."

"Yes, thank you. I'd love to do that. I never did that before."

Sofia was not interested in the conversation, but she wanted to impress me somehow.

"I hate fish and fishing. I can't bear the smell, but I do play the piano and I enjoy it," she said.

"What is a piano?" I enquired, filled with curiosity. They laughed hysterically and held their bellies. Their eyes were full of tears. I joined in the laughter without knowing the reason.

"No stop. Really, what is a piano? Is it a game or a toy?" I repeated, then they broke into a fit of giggling which attracted the whole household's attention.

"Oh, that was funny, Salem. It's a musical instrument and makes good music. Come with me, we have one here." Sofia dragged me inside and then she said, "Here it is!"

"Wow, it's a lovely table, nice and smooth," I added, even more confused.

Sofia giggled and said, "Then you definitely never saw a piano." She opened the cover and pulled a small chair from under the piano. She sat and then began playing with her fingers gently dancing on the keys. I was somewhat bewildered by the music as it was so alien to me. Signora Rossi came and asked the children to take me to their room to play there while she prepared dinner.

"I'll make you macaroni with spinach in a cream sauce and a salad," Signora Rossi said while looking at the three of us getting on well together. Sofia took me to their room and it was like entering a marvellous dream world. Everything was new to me and beyond my wildest imagination. Sofia showed me around the room. There were two solid beds with high wooden frames at the top. There were wardrobes with mirrors the length of the door and a dresser for Sofia and there were also bookshelves. A bedside locker was on each side of the bed with fancy lamps sitting on top of them and huge chandeliers hung from the ceiling. The children switched on the lights and the room instantly became alive and bright. To me it was as if someone had worked a miracle, as this was my first time seeing electricity in action.

"Wow, this is very nice," I said.

"Come, Salem, I'll show you my toys." Alexander waved his hand and gestured at me to follow him. There were tons of them and of every shape and size. We played for hours and for the first time in a year, I felt like a child. Only the shouting of Signora Rossi made us realise it was time for dinner.

We went straight to the washroom, as we were instructed by Signora Rossi, to wash our hands while she was lighting the candles on the dinner table. The rear and front balconies were opened which created a soft draught. Once I laid my eyes on the food, I salivated as Signora Rossi served it. The table was dressed for the occasion and fresh home-baked bread, which Signorina De Luca put on the table, she took her seat beside me. Alexander and Sofia were sitting opposite me and Signora and Signore Rossi sat at the top of the table facing each other. I learned a new custom just before we began to eat. We all held hands and Signora Rossi explained this custom.

"It's grace before meals."

Signore Rossi thanked the Lord for all the grace that was given to him and his family. Everyone closed their eyes except me and once the word "Amen" was mentioned, we began eating and passing things to each other. Signore Rossi started the conversation by asking the children what they wanted to do the next day and everybody engaged in conversation, but for the whole time, Signore Rossi acted as if I was not there.

The dinner was scrumptious. Signora Rossi truly was a great cook. After dinner the ladies brought different types of sweets and hot chocolate for us. At that time, Signore Rossi had retired to his usual place to smoke his pipe.

"*Grazie mille*, Signora Rossi," I told her while assisting in bringing the dishes to the sink.

"Salem, go and relax. Leave that to me. You will be doing a lot of that later," Signora Rossi said while taking the dishes from me. Signora Rossi let the rest of the washing up to Signorina De Luca and went inside.

Soon we got to the bedroom and we all changed into our night clothes. Sofia looked like a little princess. She sat on the chair by her dresser and combed her silky hair. Sofia was ten years old.

"Salem," Sofia called.

"Yes, Sofia?" I replied.

"I want to ask you something. It's really bothering me."

"What is it?"

"Well, my teacher and my father are always telling us that we shouldn't mix with the local Libyan kids. They say that you hate us because we're better than you are, and we are the kids of the Fascist Italy and you should be our servants. Is that true, Salem?" Sofia said this while still combing her hair and looking in the mirror.

"I don't know what you mean by fascist, but I thought the Italians hated us. They took away everything I loved, but I don't hate anyone. I just don't understand what's happening around me."

"Well, that's interesting. To be fascist is to be loyal to Il Duce, the King and Italy," she answered.

"But who is Il Duce?"

"He is Benito Mussolini, the leader of the Fascist Party and the head of the state. He is a very powerful and strong man," she said with a hint of excitement in her voice.

"Well, I don't know him, but when the Italian soldiers came to our tent in Al-agaila to take my sister Aisha away, I fought them. They were really mean and are they fascist, Sofia?"

Sofia turned and looked at me with her beautiful big eyes, but said nothing. Sofia did not know that in wars and when people are oppressed, children have no childhood. The door opened and Signorina De Luca entered carrying some bed clothes and pillows to make my bed, and as she started making my bed on the floor, then all hell broke loose outside the room.

"No, he will not sleep in the same room with my children!" Signore Rossi screamed.

Signora Rossi said that it was not fair on the little boy. "I feel ashamed of myself. Are we taking him from one misery to another?" She sounded hurt and I thought she might have been sobbing.

"I don't care, but that little Bedouin will not sleep in the same room with my kids."

"You're so damn stubborn! You helped me to get him out of there. Please let him stay, I beg you," Signora Rossi pleaded but in vain.

"Yes, I helped him to get out thinking maybe we could give him to the church to help him. I did that for you, but not for him to stay with us," Signore Rossi answered with authority.

"How can I face him? Where will he sleep tonight?" Signora Rossi cried.

"He can sleep in the kitchen tonight, but tomorrow he'll have to sleep elsewhere," Signore Rossi said then he slammed the door.

All you worry about is your friends and what they're going to say. Go to hell, you and your Il Duce!" Signora Rossi barked and wept. All that time Alexander, Sofia and I were like little kittens fearing for our lives. Signore Rossi was indeed a very mean man. Signorina De Luca was holding one of my hands, while Sofia was holding the other and tears ran down her cheeks. Alexander covered his ears with his hands as if not wanting to hear anything else. I felt empty, but my worries were for Signora Rossi. I felt bad because I wanted to say something in the woman's defence, but , there was not much I could say.

Signora Rossi came to the room still teary–eyed and said, "Come, kids. Say goodnight to Salem." My bed was made in the kitchen. Signora Rossi hugged me tight and said, "I promise you, I will never give you to anyone." My bed in Signora Rossi's kitchen was far superior to the one in Al-agaila, but I felt lonely and totally unwanted.

At dawn, the aroma from Signorina De Luca's coffee invaded the kitchen and roused me out of a deep sleep. Despite what happened the night before, I felt safe. Signorina De Luca noticed that I was awake as she heard me yawning and stretching.

"*Buongiorno*, Salem. I hope you had a good sleep," she said while dressing the table for the morning breakfast.

"*Buongiorno*, Signorina De Luca. I had a good sleep. I was just worried about Signora Rossi," I confessed while I was folding away the beddings and put them out of the way.

"Go, Salem, and freshen up. I will make you coffee with milk, boiled eggs, jam and butter," she said before switching the stove off upon the eggs being ready. It was not long before Signorina De Luca and I were at the breakfast table, engaged in a conversation while munching away.

"Listen, Salem, I want you to know that I am so sorry for the terrible ordeal that you had to go through in Al-agaila. It's a truly horrific experience that shouldn't happen to anyone," Signorina De Luca said in a somewhat sorrowful tone. I did not respond but I felt overwhelmed by Signorina De Luca's comments and I tried so hard to restrain couple of tears from escaping my eyes. She quickly changed the subject as she saw the effect of her words on me.

"I just want to tell you about Signore Rossi. He is a very difficult man to deal with and will take a long time for anyone to get through to him." She then spread butter on a piece of bread.

Signora Rossi entered the Kitchen wearing a silk nightdress; she greeted us while walking straight to a jug of freshly squeezed orange juice. She poured some into a glass and turned to ask me if I had a good sleep.

"*Si*, Signora Rossi, thank you very much. I hope you had the same," I replied while looking at her eyes, which were a bit red and tired. I thought that she must have cried for a considerable amount of time during the night, but her beauty never faded.

"I'm so sorry about what happened last night, but for me and you there is a lot to discuss," she assured me. "We will leave that until later."

By 6 o'clock the same morning, we were outside the building and it was still dark. Stars were still shining brightly above Benghazi. Streets oil lamps were dimming and the air was very fresh as the breeze touched our faces.

"This is the Italian section of the city, Salem. Here we feel like we are home. This part of the city is as much the same as any little Italian city from the Motherland," Signora Rossi explained. Every building was painted in the same colour. There were shops of all kinds and small trees lined both sides of every street.

"It won't be long now, Salem. We are nearly there," Signora Rossi said. Soon we were outside her café. There was a light inside as the wooden doors were wide open and only the glass doors were closed. Signora Rossi tapped on the glass door gently and a good–looking young lady with a small frame opened the door. Upon seeing Signora Rossi, she immediately screamed with delight and hugged her.

"*Buongiorno*, Signora Rossi! How are you? How was your trip?"

"I'm very well, thank you. The trip was rather long but worth every minute of it."

"And who is this handsome young man?" the young lady asked.

"Ah, forgive my ignorance. Salem, this is Signorina Sandra Mancini, my colleague and assistant. Sandra, this is Salem."

"*Buongiorno*, Salem. How are you?"

"*Buongiorno*, Signorina Mancini. I am fine, thank you."

"Well, I've heard a lot about you, Salem, and you're not at all what I imagined. You definitely look like a handsome Italian boy," Signorina Mancini remarked.

"Now that the introduction is out of the way, we can get on with our business." Signora Rossi put an arm around my shoulder and beckoned us inside.

Her café in some ways embodied Signora Rossi's personality with its interesting layout, and the place possessed a wonderful atmosphere. There were round tables covered in fancy Burgundy cloths and on them were candle holders and glasses. Pictures of places and people hung on the walls. I guessed that they were places and characters from Signora Rossi's Motherland. At the top was a deli with many different kinds of meat and cheeses and in the back, a counter along with a big unit stuck onto the wall in the background with all sorts of glasses and bottles. A sign with the word "Toilets" was placed above a door and there were couple of amazing chandeliers hanging overhead. I instantly fell in love with the place from the moment I saw it. We started getting the place ready for customers and I began helping Signora Rossi putting some tables outside and she gave me clean ashtrays to place on them. Then she brought out some sort of an item similar to a vehicle engine crank, but it was much longer and she showed me how to use it. It was for the canopy to block the sun for customers who sat outside.

At that time, I noticed the name of the café. It was written in very big letters,"Café de Milano". Signorina Mancini was very busy preparing coffee and the tea pots and heating up the milk. The place was very clean and ready. Signora Rossi asked her assistant to make her a cup of coffee because she wanted to chat with me before the customers started coming in.

We sat down at the front table. Signora Rossi lit up a cigarette and began by saying, "Listen carefully, Salem."

I nodded my head to show that she had my undivided attention.

"First I would like to apologise for what happened last night. Signore Rossi is very much a military man and he's so stubborn. He is not the easiest man to deal with and even I find it difficult sometimes to deal with him, but with a little time and patience, I always get around him. So, Salem, this is going to be your place where you sleep. I don't want to give you to anybody else. It's only temporary, I promise." When Signora Rossi finished, she held my hand.

"The other thing that you will be is my helper in here as Signorina Mancini is leaving in two weeks to go back to Italy for good. So we will show you everything so you can take over her duties. I really want you to be happy, Salem. I want to give you some of what you've lost. Do you understand?"

"Yes," I replied.

"I'll bring you an apron tomorrow, okay?"

The sun started to rise over the skies of Benghazi and a new chapter in my life just began. Signora Rossi suggested that we start with the toilets. She showed me both the men and women's toilets and said that I had to clean them periodically during the day and to make sure to change the towels. Then Signora Rossi opened another door and said, "Come in, Salem. This is the storeroom, this where we keep our stock."

It was a large room with many bags and boxes. There were many different types of meats and cheese hanging on strings from the ceiling. Signora Rossi explained the reason for this.

"They're hung like that, Salem, to get enough air to keep them fresh and also to be away from the reach of cats and mice, not that we have them here, but one must be careful rather than sorry." There were cases of wine and other drinks. Small windows were up near the ceiling to let in some light into the room. "So, Salem, you make sure that the room remains clean and to keep an eye on the stock and take note of the things that go low so we can order more. Always remember, Salem, that what comes first must go first. Do you understand all this?"

"*Si*, I understand."

"Okay. That is enough information for one day. Let's get on with the real work."

It was not long before the streets bustled and punters started to come in. There were a lot of greetings and salutations. The place was buzzing as the Italians are very emotional and passionate and that reflects in the way they talk.

We were like bees in a beehive, so busy, and you got no chance to stop. I learned quite quickly and I was doing almost everything from cleaning the ashtrays to taking the orders and cleaning the toilets. Signora Rossi and Signorina Mancini constantly watched me and their eyes followed me everywhere. At one stage, I heard Signorina Mancini whispering to Signora Rossi,

"He's a great worker. You won't notice that I'm gone with a helper like him around."

People were coming and going very quickly. By the afternoon, Signorina De Luca came by carrying some stuff. It was for me to make my bed in the storeroom.

"*Buongiorno* everyone," Signorina De Luca greeted us and then asked. "Where should I leave these things?"

"Go straight to the storeroom with them. Just leave the beddings there. You don't have to do anything with them," Signora Rossi replied. On the way out, Signorina De Luca did not stop but shouted that she was on her way to pick up the children from the club as they were on their summer holidays.

By 5 o'clock, the place was full and the atmosphere had mellowed. I started lighting the candles. People were now just sipping away the wine and munching on cheese and dry meat. Clouds of cigarette smoke drifted into the air and the loud talk became whispers.

Soon Signora Rossellini entered the place and the silence turned into commotion. Men took their hats off and waved them. Others were whistling and all were trying to invite her over to their table for a glass of wine. Signora Rossellini flirted back by smiling to almost every one of them. She looked fantastic.

"Buonasera everyone," Signora Rossellini greeted before she turned to me and kissed me on the cheek. "How's your first day at work, Salem?"

"Good, really good. I'm enjoying it," I answered.

"You're a charmer and know how to win the heart of your boss," Signora Rossellini commented. We all laughed and then the ladies sat at a small table in the corner. Signora Rossi asked Sandra for two glasses of wine and began a deep and quiet conversation. As for me and Signorina Mancini, we started getting the place cleaned and cleared the tables.

At 7 o'clock the place was empty. I brought in the tables from outside, folded the canopy back and swept the floors while Signorina Mancini did the rest. After about nearly half an hour of cleaning, the place was restored to the way it was in the morning. Then the two ladies went to the storeroom and made my bed. Signora Rossi called me and showed me it.

"Salem, my heart is aching and I feel ashamed, but it's the only way that I can keep you safe and under my protection for now at least," Signora Rossi explained in a browbeaten tone.

"It's the truth, Salem. Signora Rossi loves you but the circumstances aren't in her favour," Signora Rossellini added.

"You don't have to worry about anything. I am so pleased and so grateful to you both. Any place will be a million times better than Al-agaila. I have no one except you." As I said those last words, Signora Rossi fell to her knees and began sobbing. Signora Rossellini placed her friend's head on her shoulder and calmed her.

"You shouldn't be too hard on yourself. What you're doing is great and Salem is so grateful. So you should be strong," Signora Rossellini said. Signora Rossi wiped her tears and then turned to me.

"Well, Salem, this bag is yours. It has your pyjamas and some clothes and a change of underwear for you. There's also other stuff to clean yourself with." Then Signora Rossi lit a candle for me and put it up on a shelf as the room had no light. It made the room look safer.

"Grazie mille, Signora Rossi. Everything will be all right. You go now, I will be fine," I assured her. I walked with them to the main room and they all wished me a good night's sleep.

Just before she left, Signora Rossi pointed at a table and said, "This is your dinner. You must eat it before you sleep, and don't forget to switch off the lights here before you go to bed." When they were outside, Signorina Mancini closed the glass doors and locked them with keys and as they started pulling the folding wooden doors, they were looking at me with eyes full of sympathy. The doors were now completely closed and the rattling of the keys had stopped. I felt that my heart stopped with it. For the first time, I was going to be alone, and I would sleep in a place with no one around me. I learned later that loneliness is worse than dying.

After a long day and racked with tiredness, I went straight to the storeroom, changed into my pyjamas, cleaned myself up and ate my dinner. To my surprise, it was macaroni with cream and cheese with homemade bread and a glass of warm milk. I devoured it in no time, and then suddenly a weird and sombre feeling washed over me. I remembered the whole thing from the arrival of the Italians to our village to the time that Signora Rossi came to rescue me. Tears just ran down my face and I found myself asking God, "Why did all the people I love have to go?"

My only response was silence. Once I washed the plate, my thoughts returned to Signora Rossi, and I told myself that she will eventually persuade Signore Rossi to allow me to move into the house. Sofia and Alexander had made me feel like a child once again. These thoughts changed my mood and I was overwhelmed with a sort of warm, loving feeling. For once, I did not feel like a little dog that wags his tail when he sees his master. This made me remember my dog, Saiyad. Once I finished drying the dishes, I switched the lights off, but the minute I did that, everything went into total darkness. The darkness scared me so I turned on the light immediately.

How will I make it to the storeroom without the light? This was the question I asked myself. Then the answer came. The only way was to open the door to the toilets and then open the store door so that the candle light would guide me to my bed. It worked.

Without any delay, I went straight to my little bed and tucked myself in. The bed was very comfortable. I was tired and my muscles ached. My eyes were focused on the ceiling and the lines of cheese and dry meat. Then I thought about all the boys back in the concentration camp and suddenly a shadow, an actual moving shadow appeared on the wall! It morphed into various shapes and I was convinced that it was definitely a ghost. This was the one that my grandfather used to tell me about. My hands held the edge of my quilt so tightly and my heart pounded like a drum. I tried to scream and I called my father, mother, Aisha, Sidi Rajab and Signora Rossi, but somehow the words never left my mouth. I whimpered and as the flame of the candle danced about, the shape of everything in the room began to appear on the wall. I managed to cover my head but then old memories haunted me. The screaming of Aisha when she was taken away by those brutal soldiers and the weeping of my mother for her, and the sound of guns being discharged on the march to hell. I thought I was going to die by smothering myself. I needed air and very quickly, so I mustered every ounce of inner strength and managed to move the cover slowly from over my head. I felt a touch of a breeze and took a deep breath. I recited every verse I knew from the Quran. I was so exhausted, and like magic, my eyes closed and slipped into a deep sleep.

Dawn arrived as the voice of the orator from a far away mosque announced that prayer time had arrived. I opened my eyes and the candle had quenched. I stayed in bed for a little while contemplating about the night before and told myself that it was nothing but my overactive imagination. Having thought it over, I decided not to tell anyone for I thought that they might think I was only looking for sympathy and a way out of this. Any sign of weakness on my part would put tremendous pressure on Signora Rossi so I had to remain strong.

Soon the morning light crept in slowly through those small windows near the ceiling. I jumped out of my bed and went straight to the bathroom to freshen up. Then I returned to make the bed and changed into my working clothes. I switched on the lights in the main room and I began preparing the place for the ladies for when they came in. Then I sat by the table near the door, I heard footsteps from time to time and people talking.

"Signorina Mancini will be here soon," I told myself. Few minutes later I heard The sound of rattling keys outside the doopr. It was Signorina Mancini and I felt a sense of relief.

"Buongiorno, Salem. You're very early. Did you have a good night's sleep?"

"Buongiorno, Signorina Mancini. Grazie, I really did have a good night's sleep, and I was up with the chanticleers."

"Wow, that early?" Signorina Mancini said with a face full of admiration. We started getting on with our job. I put the tables outside and placed the ashtrays on them, lowered the canopy and gave the floor a quick sweep. Then Signora Rossi entered and after the greeting, she ran toward me and gave me a big hug.

"Oh, I was so worried about you all night. I was thinking of coming over to check on you. I felt terrible for having to put you through this," Signora Rossi said while smoothing down my face with her hands.

"Don't worry, I'm fine. Thank you for taking me out of Al-agaila."

"You're one beautiful, brave boy," Signora Rossi said after planting a warm kiss on my forehead.

It was another busy day, and when Signora Rossi closed the shop that evening, I was scared more than ever. My dinner was on the table and it was something that Signora Rossi had brought from home. I sat down and ate my dinner, but the images of last night and the dark thoughts infiltrated my mind. After finishing the dinner, I was unable to move and the horrifying thoughts of going to bed terrified me. In the end, I came to the conclusion that there was no other way out of this but to simply go to the storeroom and face my fears. I tried to convince myself that the images from the night before were nothing but a figment of my imagination.

Once the usual routine was completed, I closed the door behind me and within seconds I was under the bed cover. The flame on the wick danced and all the objects in the storeroom started appearing on the wall. My whole body was covered. I was fixated with the shadow on the wall and to my dismay, it soon morphed into a sort of ghost that moved in slow motion. Suddenly I heard my heart beating furiously and I started shivering. My forehead was drenched with sweat and I was numb. Each attempt to close my eyes ended in failure. The shadow appeared and disappeared and I thought that the ghost was playing tricks on me. From his shadowy body, I saw that it had big ears. Having momentarily quelled the trepidation inside of me, I braved a glance around the place to scan every corner of it and to my surprise and relief, the dreadful ghost was nothing but a tiny mouse. Once that discovery had been made, it felt as if a ton had been lifted off my chest. My body was no longer rigid or tense and now I could move my head to see where the little creature went. He was surreptitiously moving from one place to another as he sensed my presence. Without thinking, I got out of bed and went straight to the deli in the main room and took a small slice of cheese and returned to my bed. Now all my fears had been transformed into excitement. I placed small little pieces beside my bed and waited for the mouse. Then he appeared and I knew that no mouse in the world could resist the smell of cheese. His movements were methodical and its nose worked hard to locate it. Finally the mouse got to the first one and began munching away on it.

As it neared me, I became more and more excited. Soon my tiny companion was only a few centimetres away. The little mouse became unafraid as it did not react to my movement. Then I decided to put one piece into my hand and place my hand on the floor to see if I could lure the mouse into my palm. It worked and he was on my palm, eating the cheese. He was white on some parts of his body but I figured very quickly that was because he lived between the flour cases. When he was finished, he looked at me with his deep, sharp little black eyes and I gave him a name. It was "Formaggio", and from that moment onwards, Formaggio was my little friend who helped me cope with the lonely nights in the storeroom. I lowered my hand and let Formaggio slip gently onto the floor. I gave him my last piece of cheese and watched him eat it. I felt so safe and content that my eyes were becoming heavier and I was unable to resist the power of sleep. Soon I dreamt of funny monsters and silly ghosts.

When I woke up early in the morning, Formaggio was gone and there were no traces of cheese. I smiled before going into my usual little routine. The rattling of the keys was a sign that either Signora Rossi or Signorina Mancini was about to enter. I was full of energy and in a very good mood.

"*Buongiorno*, Salem," Signorina Mancini greeted me while yawning.

"*Buongiorno*, Signorina Mancini. I had a good night's sleep. Did you?"

"Don't ask, Salem. It was a very late night. We went to the Inn of Signore Murdoch. We had quite a few."

I did not fully understood her, but I continued the conversation by telling her about my good night's sleep.

"Wow, Salem, you seem to acclimatise very well and quickly with this place. You are so brave, Salem. I have to give you that as I can't stay on my own. I don't know how you do it!"

Signorina Mancini did not really know the terrifying ordeal that I had to go through in the last couple of nights, but I managed to stick with it. Signora Rossi appeared twenty minutes later looking so tired and in a very quiet mood. She handed me a bag with my little apron and Italian cap. She asked me to put them on and the ladies were very amused at how I looked.

"You look like a professional waiter," Signorina Mancini remarked.

The day was like the one before, very busy, and there was a great buzz around the place. I must say I started to enjoy it and as time went on, I learned the trade very quickly because I knew that Signora Rossi would be counting on me to run the café with her. Over time, I became quite familiar with the customers and their personalities. As for Signorina Mancini, the excitement of going back to the mainland and getting married began to become a reality and was getting closer by the minute. The fortnight went very quickly and my friendship with Formaggio grew stronger. Saturday arrived and it was the last night of Signorina Mancini's three-year period as a worker in this café. Signora Rossi had made arrangements earlier in the week with her friends to come to the café this Saturday to take Signorina Mancini out and give her a good send off. That day Sandra told me about how happy she was in going back to Italy. She said that they had a little farm in the south of Italy and they may stay there and raise a family, but there were tears in her eyes as she spoke about how she was going to miss Benghazi.

At 7 o'clock, Signora, Delveccio and the glamorous Signora Rossellini arrived. They were carrying presents for Signorina Mancini. Signora Rossi offered them a drink and went to the bathroom along with Sandra to get ready for the dinner party. After a little while, they came back looking very fresh and well dressed. They shared a few glasses of wine and got into a fun mood. As for me, I was busy having my dinner that Signora Rossi brought with her. It was delicious. Anything that Signora Rossi ever made was always a pleasure to eat.

After one hour or so, the ladies started getting ready to go out. I stood up to say farewell to Signorina Mancini, but she placed her hands on my shoulders and knelt down so her face was directly opposite mine.

"I really enjoyed the last two weeks and I learned a lot from you, Salem. I will always have a place in my heart for you."

"Thanks for being nice to me and for showing me what to do here. I'll miss you too," I replied and then we hugged. All the other ladies were wiping their tears. Seconds later, the café was completely shut and I was alone, but since my discovery of little Formaggio, fear never entered my heart again in that place.

The next day I got a little surprise. While I was sitting at the front table listening to the people going by, I heard a rattling of keys. Someone was trying to open the door.

This is unusual, I thought. It's a Sunday and it's the day that Signora Rossi doesn't open the café. Then the wooden door was folded and Signora Rossi and the kids appeared. It felt like seeing my own family again. When Sigora Rossi opened the second door, I could not resist hugging her. Sofia and Alexander were looking very sharp and immaculate and they were very happy to see me.

"We just got back from the church," Signora Rossi said while she was making her way into the café.

"I'm so glad to see you guys again. Did you forget something, Signora Rossi?" I asked.

"No, Salem, we came especially for you. We came to take you home with us. You're going to spend the night at our house. Come on, let's get your stuff," Signora Rossi said. Understandably, I did not hang about and got everything.

"I'm going to take the bed cover, pillow cases and all your dirty laundry to replace them with new ones," Signora Rossi told me. From that moment on, Sunday became a day that I spent with the Rossi family and the day that I got my hot bath. It was also on Sunday nights that I played with the Rossi children, feeling like a child once again. But before leaving the café on Saturday evening, I always made sure that a good chunk of cheese was left for Formaggio.

CHAPTER FIFTEEN

Rumours were spreading rapidly in the Piazza that Sidi Omar's days were numbered and "Fat Toni" was the one who spreading the rumours. The departure of Signorina Mancini did not make my job any easier but gave me the chance to mingle with the customers more and I got to know their names. It was September, Sofia and Alexander returned to school. I got to see them almost every morning when they passed by the café.

A peculiar thing occurred also in that month and it was the arrival of new Libyan customers; young men, who dressed like the Italians, combed their hair in the same style and refused to speak in anything else but Italian. They were damn good at it too. They were the Libyans who joined the Italian movement, which was similar in its principles of the Fascist Party back in Rome and as Signora Rossi told me, these men were working in the Italian establishments in Benghazi. They were in their early 30s, but the ones who stood out were, Faouzi, Dawood and Najeeb, and that is because every time they ate or drink in the café , they were invariably involved in some debate with Fat Toni that always ended up in a quarrel, and most of the time required the intervention of Signora Rossi to defuse the intense situation.

"If you calm down, you will have a drink on the house," Signora Rossi used to say and that worked every time. Fat Toni, or to give him his full name, Toni Maltese, was the owner of the butchers shop nearby and had a large, rotund belly. He was a regular, and without difficulty, guzzled down three bottles of wine in any given day. The newspaper never left his hands as he used it well when talking. Toni waved it in so many different directions and he was a funny guy. But his favourite times were when the Libyan lads are there, he always said something in hope that it would ignite a conversation with them, fuelled with aggressiveness and prejudice. Deep down, however, he was a soft man with a kind heart as he always bought them a drink.

"Roma needs the likes of you to have any chance to remain in this land. Look, read the paper. Nobody reads the paper anymore!" Fat Tony exclaimed, waving his paper over his head. Sometimes when he was unsuccessful in getting the lads' attention, he resorted to different tactics. "The brave Graziani, the Champion of Rome, has captured the spectacles of Omar Al-Mukhtar and soon he'll catch him and break his neck," Toni taunted, throwing his paper across the room.

"This will never happen, you know, as long as Italy doesn't fulfil its promises and give the people what they want. People will always support Al-Mukhtar," Dawoud answered back sternly. Toni sat there with a big smile and some sort of delightful expression of satisfaction that his trick had worked again.

"You are the ones who don't respect treaties and you never fulfil your promises. Look at the Sonousi and Omar, they are like mercury, you can never put your hand on it. They are nothing but dirty rats and sordid Bedouins!" Tony aimed the paper directly at Faouzi to get him in the conversation while throwing down his throat a big measure from his wine glass. I could not believe what I was hearing. He called them Beduoins as he tried to insult them.

"For your information, they are Bedouins. Look at you, Toni, you were as poor as a church mouse before you came here," Faouzi replied infuriated. As Faouzi finished his comment, I could not help but laugh.

Suddenly Fat Toni moved his attention toward me and shouted to Signora Rossi, "You don't know what you're doing. You're grooming and feeding a young Bedouin, but once he becomes a man, he'll turn against us and follow in the footsteps of Omar Al-Mukhtar!"

Then I moved toward him and said, "Signora Rossi will give you a free bottle of wine if you can see your feet while standing up straight."

Fat Toni paused for a second and then he started screaming, using all sorts of foul language. The whole place erupted in laughter and Signora Rossi sent a free glass of wine to everyone.

That was the kind of atmosphere which continued day in and day out.

Signora Rossi was bringing me different books every week and used to spend time with me after work, teaching me proper Italian. Sunday was the day that I waited all week for. Sofia, Alexander and I formed a great friendship. Even though Signore Rossi had agreed with his wife that she could bring me on Sundays, I was still very afraid of him, especially when he was in uniform. I think it was because it reminded me of Al-agaila and I always tried to avoid eye contact with him. As for my friend Formaggio, he started responding to my voice and to his name. I must say that he became a little overweight and sometimes I called him "Fatso", I stopped calling him that and also lessened his food.

Despite adapting well to the new life, new culture and language, I still thought strongly of the things that meant a lot to me, even though they were nothing but memories at that stage of my young life. There was not one day or night that passed by that I did not think or pray for the people in the camp. I prayed for their ordeal to soon be over and that I would meet with them once again to tell them about my little adventure with Formaggio and the Rossi family. One of the things that constantly hurt me the most was the night Aisha was taken away. I vowed that when I was older, I would search for her, even if it took me far across the sea. It often amazes me how I coped with it back then, but Sidi Rajab's words always came to mind, "The orphans have the Lord himself watching over them."

* * *

The morning passed slowly and progressed into a fabulous sunny afternoon as the sun lit up the hills of the Green Mountain and the nearby regions with its glorious rays. An aroma of wild sage and thyme wafted past Sidi Omar's nose. It was the eleventh day of September 1931. Horses' hooves trotted on the rocky valley of Butaga. Horsemen were appearing and disappearing

behind the trees of Albattoum and Alshemari which covered
the Green Mountain all year round. The Green Mountains and
its valleys had given Sidi Omar cover and shelter for the last 20
years against his formidable enemy, the Italians.

Sidi Omar was coming back from a secret meeting with
fighters from different camps and he had learned that an Italian
unit was moving toward the village of Slunta. He was about to
put together a plan to ambush the unit, as they were desperate
for food and ammunition. Sidi Omar and his men were heading
to an inescapable death, as the Italians learned from their
informers that Omar Al-Mukhtar was in Slunta.

"We will make camp here just for couple of hours to get some
rest and inspect our guns," Sidi Omar ordered his men.

"Good spot, Sidi Omar," Sidi Hammed agreed.

"Listen, Hammed, give orders to the men that no fire shall
be lit nor shall any cigarettes be smoked. We mustn't give the
enemy any chance to discover our presence," Sidi Omar warned.

"Yes, Sidi Omar, at once." Sidi Hammed departed to relay
the orders.

Men dismounted from their horses and there were about sixty
men in total. The deplorable measures that General Graziani
had taken to deprive Omar Al-Mukhtar's men of provisions had
taken its toll.

"Bourheel, where are you?" Sidi Omar called out.

"I'm here, Sidi Omar."

"Send few men to locate the whereabouts of the Italian
unit and ask them to get some indication of their numbers and
weapons. And put some men up on those hills."

"At once," Bourheel replied.

"Abdul Hamid, come closer to me. It's our golden opportunity
to motivate our men and boost their morale. We have lost many
men lately. We need successes in this operation and we need
food and ammunition," Sidi Omar explained.

"Inshallah, we will be victorious."

"Yes, inshallah. Tell the men to be vigilant. I'm going to pray
for a while."

"Pray for us, Sidi Omar," Sidi Abdul Hamid replied.

Sidi Omar Al-Mukhtar, now aged 73, sat in deep concentration, praying with all his might while the men were cleaning their guns and reloading them.

A couple of hours later, the young men returned from their reconnaissance.

"Sidi Bourheel, they're at our mercy. We can take them by surprise. They're definitely carrying provisions and ammunition to one of their camps. It's our chance to survive a little longer," the young man reported back.

"You've done a great job," Sidi Bourheel replied. "How many of them are there?"

"There are about one hundred soldiers and about twenty horsemen," the other young fighter revealed.

Sidi Omar called upon all the men to gather around him as he knelt down and began explaining his plan and how to attack swiftly but in a devastating manner. He was making circles, lines and crosses by drawing on the ground with a branch, talking and giving each one a different role.

Unknown to Sidi Omar, for the first time in 20 years he was walking into a trap, the one he used so well to frustrate the Italians in a lightning raid.

Sidi Omar and his men commenced their journey toward the Butaga valley. Suddenly the sound of gunfire broke the deadly silence.

"They're attacking us from behind. It's a trap! We have been ambushed!" Sidi Omar shouted.

"Protect Sidi Omar," one man yelled. Some of Sidi Omar's men were hit within the first minute, but soon they turned and valiantly charged at the Italians.

"They're retreating! It's our chance. Let's follow them, they will not escape from us," another man urged.

"Bourheel, stay with few men. Try to shelter those who got wounded and then follow us towards Wadi El Kouf," Sidi Abdul Hamid commanded.

The Italians knew exactly the whereabouts of Sidi Omar and his men. They had been monitoring the situation from the night before and then set their trap. They were luring them to exactly where they wanted them to be. A unit waited in Wadi El Kouf while another unit took them by surprise from behind.

Al-Mukhtar was now totally surrounded by Italian troops and running out of ammunition.

"We are trapped," Sidi Hamid said.

"Where is Sidi Omar? Where is he?" Sidi Hamad asked.

Sidi Omar's name was echoing throughout the valleys of the Green Mountains. The Italians hit them with everything they had.

"There is an escape route, men. There! Try to escape through it!" Sidi Omar informed his soldiers.

Without warning, Al-Mukhtar's horse was hit and he fell to the ground, receiving wounds to his leg.

"Sidi Omar has been hit!" one man roared. Then the Italian officer gave an order to cease fire. The remainder of Sidi Omar's men sought a chance to flee and this they did.

News of Sidi Omar's capture spread like wildfire. It was a sad day for the whole region of Barka and for Libya. Italian soldiers, upon hearing that Omar had been hit, advanced slowly to Sidi Omar's position. He was lying on the ground with injuries to his leg sustained by falling from his horse. Twenty soldiers and a few officers surrounded Al-Mukhtar, training their weapons on him. An informer came and had a look at Sidi Omar and verified that this man was indeed Al-Mukhtar, but the Italians wanted to be sure before declaring that the leader of the rebels had been captured. In order to do this, they had to get the only Italian man that could identify Sidi Omar: Signore Daowud Alyatchi. He was known to the people of the Green Mountain and he preferred to be called this because he was married to a Libyan woman.

* * *

Signore Daowud was at his office when he received the news. He knew Al-Mukhtar very well as he was the mediator between the Italians and the rebels. One soldier entered his office and saluted him.

"What is the matter?" Signor Alyatchi asked.

"We have received news that Al-Mukhtar is captured."

Startled, yet somewhat filled with excited disbelief, Signore Alyatchi stood up and shouted, "Where and when?" he asked.

"This afternoon, Signore, in the valley of Butaga in Slunta."

"Great news!" Signore Alyatchi replied. "Prepare my plane at once and send the news to Rome. General Graziani must be informed."

General Graziani was in Italy on an official visit and also attended a military show in Paris. When the news came, he cancelled all his arrangements and took his private airplane back to Benghazi.

Signore Alyatchi's arrival was met by officers who captured Sidi Omar and took him straight to his cell. When Signore Alyatchi entered, Sidi Omar was shackled.

"Omar!" Signore Alyatchi called to get Sidi Omar's attention.

Sidi Omar raised his eyes to meet Dawoud's and saluted him politely. "It has been a while since we last saw each other. You look great," Omar remarked.

"*Si*, you have aged a lot, Omar," Signore Alyatchi replied.

"It's inescapable," Sidi Omar answered.

"We always knew that we would get you in the end. It was only a matter of time."

"I'm not afraid of death. Its shadow was always hanging around me but the struggle will continue."

"No, Omar, you're the only one who can motivate the men to fight us," Signore Alyatchi replied, hoping to destroy Omar's confidence.

"We will fight you generation after generation. There is no right for a nation to occupy another."

Signore Alyatchi looked at Sidi Omar with great respect and turned to one of the officers. "Yes, this is definitely Omar Al-Mukhtar, and still as stubborn as ever. I can sign all the necessary papers."

"What's the arrangement for moving him to Benghazi?" one officer enquired.

"It's being taken care of. The best way is through the sea; this way we can avoid the rebels and the people of the Green Mountain. We cannot afford to make any mistakes now. Take him to Sousa and from there, the frigate *Orsini* will take him to Benghazi."

"Si, Signore."

"Omar, do you need anything before I go?" Signore Alyatchi asked.

"Yes, Dawoud, will you ask the officer to bring me some water and take these chains off so I can perform my prayer?"

"No, this is impossible. We can't do that, Signore," the officer replied.

Signore Alyatchi came to Omar's aid. "Omar is a very old man and wounded. He can't escape. Besides, he's a man of his word. Do what he asked at once, Officer. I will see you in Benghazi, Omar."

"Inshallah, with God's willingness. Grazie, Dawoud, you're a good man."

* * *

At the break of dawn on 12 September 1931, Sidi Omar Al-Mukhtar was sitting on the deck of the frigate *Orsini* as it set sail. Sidi Omar gazed at the Green Mountains disappearing in the horizon for the last time. He was bidding farewell to the place he loved so much.

Chapter Sixteen

Dawn was greeted by the chanticleers and by the orator of the mosque. It seemed like something big was happening in the Piazza in the early hours of the morning. There was singing, and the honking of car horns deprived us from an extra hour of sleep. By that I mean Formaggio and I. I sat on my bed until my eyes adapted to the darkness of the room.

There was a ladder in the corner. With a bit of struggle I managed to move it toward one of the small windows high up near the ceiling. I climbed its steps very carefully and upon reaching the top, I cleaned the dust with my hands. To my surprise, the Piazza was full of people carrying Italian flags and lots of drunk soldiers singing some fascist tunes. There were women and children waving and shouting "Glory to Roma and Graziani" from their balconies.

"This is huge. Something big must have happened," I muttered to myself while making my way down. Even Formaggio could not handle the commotion so he disappeared very quickly behind the flour bags. I had so many questions, but there was no one to ask so the only way to find out was to wait for Signora Rossi to come and she would inform me.

I began preparing the café for another busy day because I was wide-awake and full of energy. I did not know how long but it was quite a while before I heard the rattling of Signora Rossi's keys in the keyhole and the noise started to get louder as she opened the second door. There were many people on the street and it seemed that more and more people were flocking to the square. I was there to greet her.

"*Buongiorno*, Signora Rossi. I couldn't sleep with all the noise. What's going on?"

"*Buongiorno*, Salem. Omar Al-Mukhtar has been captured and now he is on his way to the port of Benghazi, coming from Sousa by the sea. The news came rather late last night. He should arrive sometime this afternoon, I guess," Signora Rossi explained without making any fuss about it. Signora Rossi predicted that we would be so busy that we would not have a minute to ourselves so she suggested that we should have a quick breakfast before the invasion, as she described it. Soon we were sitting at the table having our breakfast.

"Do you know what it means now, Salem? It means we can live in peace together. Don't you think so?" she asked.

"*Si*, Signora Rossi," I replied, but the truth of the matter was that I did not understand the full scale of the tragedy until I got a bit older. I learned that in wars there is never any winner. A lot of Libyan men became soldiers, but not by choice. Some joined the Allies and many fought in the desert with the Germans while others joined the Italian regiments. None of them ever knew why, and what they were fighting for. One simple but terrible fact always remains that children are the true victims of every war.

"Salem, eat. We won't be able to even get a chance to have a sip of water. We will be so busy today," Signora Rossi said while handing me another piece of pie.

Once we finished eating, we opened the doors and the customers flooded in. The customers were made up of soldiers who were out on the town, and most of them were accompanied by women, some owners of shops nearby, the Libyan crowd and of course, Fat Toni. The place was brimming with a lively and exciting atmosphere and the orders never stopped flowing in. Couple of hours later, Signora Rossi and I were sweating. The usual debate had started between Fat Toni and the Libyan lads, and the soldiers were singing and glorifying Il Duce and Graziani. Others talked about the capture of Sidi Omar. The smell of wine and tobacco was overwhelming. I was constantly changing the ashtrays and serve the tables with plates of cheese, dry meats, olives and other different dips and homemade bread. We had to go to the storeroom so many times to get more stock. The women were passing comments to me every time I got near their tables. Signora Rossi called me back, saying that we could use some extra hand. Then some men began whistling and after I turned around, I could see why. Signora Rossellini arrived and Signora Rossi's prayers had been answered.

"Hi, you're certainly busy. Wow, I've never seen the place this chaotic," Signora Rossellini said, but before she finished, Signora Rossi gave her Sandra's apron and asked her to get stuck in. Soon. I noticed that Signora Rossellini was giving extra attention to the Libyan lads and flirting a lot with Dawoud. I was shocked when later I found out that he was her lover and having an affair for quite a while.

In the afternoon, school kids with their Italian flags were out in the streets joining the crowd. Everyone began moving toward the seaport, hoping to get a glimpse of the man who had deprived the Italians of peace.

By 6 o'clock, the commotion in the café eased off and soon became very quiet. We started getting the dishes clean and everything back the way it was that morning. Signora Rossi asked me to shut the door and put up the sign (Closed) as we could not take any more customers because the normal closing time was approaching, we cleaned up the café and prepared it for the next day. At 8 o'clock, the party in the streets continued while Signora Rossi and Signora Rossellini prepared some food in the kitchen as we were starving. Soon, the three of us were sitting and enjoying our late dinner.

"I was so thrilled when I heard the news this morning," Signora Rossellini said while taking a big sip from her glass of wine.

"Yes, it's great news. I told Salem that maybe it's a new beginning for everyone. I hope we can all enjoy a permanent peace. I am so delighted for my husband and also for those people in the concentration camps. I hope this will end their suffering and get them their freedom," Signora Rossi added. Then the ladies talked about where they would go for few drinks.

As soon as I finished my food, I cleaned the remainder of the dishes. I told Signora Rossi that I would start cleaning the toilets and give the place a good wipe.

"No, Salem, you can leave that for the morning. You had a rather hard day. You deserve a good rest and an early sleep," Signora Rossi insisted.

"I'd rather do it now. We will be busy again tomorrow." I did not wait for her to respond. The toilets were very messy, but after half an hour, they were like new. I brought the bucket and mop to the main café area and started wiping the floor, and put the chairs out of the way by placing them on top of the tables. Both women were sipping away on the wine and talking. Their eyes were focused entirely on me. Then Signora Rossi went to the money drawer, took out all the takings, and placed the money on the table. She began counting it and Signora Rossellini was giving her a hand by writing down the amounts.

"Wow!" Signora Rossi exclaimed. "This is the best day we ever had since we opened few years ago."

"It was very busy and you deserve a night to chill out," Signora Rossellini replied with enthusiasm.

I was so delighted for Signora Rossi. She looked at me and said,"You're my lucky charm. Since your arrival we never had a bad day."

Once I finished the floor, I went straight to the bathroom, cleaned myself and returned to finish my glass of milk. By that time the ladies were about to go to the restroom to freshen themselves up and change their outfits for the occasion. After a little while, they came out looking like they never worked a single minute that day. Their appearance just amazed me as they looked smartly dressed and smelled wonderful.

"Well, we have to leave you now. I have lit the candle for you, I shall see you early in the morning. *Buonanotte*," Signora Rossi said before kissing me on the forehead. Then Signora Rossellini leaned down a bit and kissed me on the cheek.

"You will be very handsome man," she told me.

"*Buonanotte*, and be careful with the money. You're carrying a lot of it," I replied.

"You're truly a good boy, Salem. Don't worry, I will go to the house for a few minutes to make sure that the kids are all right, and I will leave it in the safe," Signora Rossi assured me.

"Okay then, *arrivaderci*, and *buona fortuna*!" Once the door was closed, then I heard the sound of the keys rattling, the sound that I dreaded by night, yet I loved this sound in the morning.

At that moment one thing was on my mind and one thing only: to get a piece of cheese to feed Formaggio and hit the bed as I was exhausted. I changed into my comfortable clothes and got into my bed. I called
Formaggio twice before he came running to me.

"Come to me, my good friend. I've missed you. Look what I have for you, fat piece of cheese."

Formaggio crept into my hand.

"You're alone in this world like me, young but with no family, but we have each other. You really make my staying here easier." Then I put him beside me on the floor and I gave him the rest of the cheese to finish. He was looking at me from time to time and I felt like that he was thanking me and telling me that I made his life easier too. Later in life I realised that humans need to belong to something when facing circumstances like mine. We need to be attached to something in order to continue living and making sense of life and things around us.

My eyes became too heavy to keep open and soon I was asleep. That night, I had weird dreams as I dreamt of Sidi Omar, and he appeared like a giant hero from my grandfather's tales.

The next morning Signora Rossi made it on time but she was not feeling well.

"*Buongiorno*, Salem. I'm sorry. I'm not in a good shape this morning. It was a late night and full of drama. Sit down, Salem. I will make you breakfast. I need to sit down as well." Signora Rossi held her head with her left hand.

"Is there anything I can do to help you?"

"Oh nothing at all, thank you. I shouldn't get any sympathy, Salem. It's self–inflicted. This is not what's upsetting me, Salem. It's my husband, can you believe that he ignored me all night? He was laughing with his friends and dancing with other women. He didn't ask me once to dance!" Signora Rossi cried, I handed her a table napkin.

"I'm sorry, but I thought you and Signora Rossellini were going somewhere alone," I enquired.

"That is what we did. That was the idea, but we went to this new place in Jelyana. It's really nice and most ladies go there but when we got there, he was already in with his friends, but he wouldn't acknowledge me. His excuse was that he never liked my friend." Signora Rossi looked so sad and hurt.

"Do you mean Signora Rossellini?"

"*Si*, he never liked her. He always said that she's a bad influence on me, but you should see his friends; nothing but drunken idiots," Signora Rossi added.

"Maybe if you wash your face it might help. Don't cry, Signora Rossi," I begged.

"I'm sorry, Salem, to put you through this. That wasn't fair on you." Signora Rossi washed her face and we opened the place. "Only the morning will be busy but not the afternoon. Everyone wants to go and see Omar Al-Mukhtar. It's his trial today."

"Why do all Italians hate him? Is he a bad man?"

"Well, no, I mean yes, he kills our soldiers and deprives us of peace in Cyrenaica," Signora Rossi answered but not convincingly.

"The Italian soldiers took my father, mother, grandfather and my only sister. Do you think they are bad people?" I felt that he was not the one who should be on trial.

"Come here, my little boy. I'm sorry for everything. Sometimes I feel ashamed to be Italian." Signora Rossi hugged me so tight with tears in her eyes. "Salem, you have to know that I am not in favour of the war and I don't agree with what they're doing to the natives. That's why I strived to get you out of the camp. I had no choice. I fell in love with a soldier, he was a young officer in the Italian army in the region of Milano and, against the will of my parents, I married him. I couldn't stay there. I had to come with him, and I must say that this land brought us happiness and a small share of wealth. Then we had Sofia and Alexander and they fulfilled the joy we sought in this life. But deep down I miss my parents, brothers, sisters and my home."

I hugged her and said, "Don't be sad. I'm glad you're here and thanks for taking me out of Al-agaila." I even made her laugh when I told her, "Why don't you go visit your family after we close the shop?"

It was as exactly as Signora Rossi predicted; we were very busy in the morning but business died down by the afternoon. There were only few people coming and going. By around 5 o'clock, the Libyan crowd arrived and took the table near the door, asking for the usual bottle of wine.

It's a good thing that Fat Toni isn't around today, I thought, otherwise Signora Rossi will go mad. She was still hung over and held her head few times.

An hour later, Signora Rossellini arrived and, as always, looked stunning. She stopped first to talk to Dawoud and told him that she would see him tonight. Then she came toward us. "*Buonasera*. You're not as busy as I thought. I think the whole town has gone to see Al-Mukhtar," she said.

"That's true. Come, let's sit down and have a drink," Signora Rossi said while making her way to the table.

"How is my little boy today? You look as handsome as ever," Signora Rossellini commented.

"*Grazie mille*. What should I get you?" I asked.

"Ah, a bottle of red wine" Signora Rossi ordered.

"Do you want the usual red wine, Signora?" I asked.

"*Si, please*" Signora Rossi replied.

Soon I came back with two glasses and a bottle of wine for them and then I added, "Do you really love getting headaches, Signora Rossi?"

The ladies laughed, then Signora Ross said "You're funny and cheeky Salem."

Having served the boss her wine, I started getting the tables ready once again and for the first time while changing the ashtray for the lads, I got to talk to them and they could not believe my Italian was so good. They were shocked when I told them that I was a prisoner in the concentration camp of Al-agaila. I also told them that Signora Rossi rescued me after I lost my whole family. They both stared at me with a look of sympathy but also admiration.

"You are some boy, aren't you?" Faouzi said. They put their hands into their pockets to get some change for me but I told them there was no need. Signora Rossi looked after me well.

"Do you want anything else?" I asked. There was a little pause before they asked for the bill. I asked Signora Rossi to do their bill while I cleared their table. Dawoud seized the opportunity and moved toward Signora Rossellini, snatching a quick kiss. They said their goodbyes and were the last customers to leave.

Soon after they left, Signora Rossi told me to shut the shop. I sorted everything and then sat down to my dinner. Signora Rossi always made sure that my dinner was ready at closing time. Sometimes she brings me food from house and other times she prepared food for me in the café. I took a table away from the two ladies even though they asked me to sit at theirs. I declined, however, I did not want to listen to their private conversation.

Only two minutes into my dinner and Signora Rossi was crying again. As one would expect, Signora Rossellini was very supportive. After finishing my dinner, I started giving the floor a good wipe. Then Signora Rossellini lit a few candles and switched the light off.

An hour later, Signora Rossi was getting ready and changing into a different outfit. "Signora Rossellini and I are going out for the night.

"I'll make you forget about your sadness tonight. You will have the time of your life and I'll find you a handsome Libyan man," Signora Rossellini promised with a devilish giggle.

"You're crazy. I can never imagine myself cheating on Bruno," Signora Rossi replied while looking at herself in a compact mirror.

"I don't call it cheating. I call it a bit of fun. You have to make him realise what he's missing. You have to make him realise that you can do exactly the same thing he did last night and with a very handsome young man," Signora Rossellini told her in an authoritative tone.

"He has been ignoring me lately. Between his work and friends, he has no time for me. We seldom go out. I mean, he hasn't asked me out for a long time. We haven't eaten in a restaurant in months. He hasn't bought a present for me in ages, not even flowers," Signora Rossi revealed while sobbing.

"All men are the same." Signora Rossellini confirmed her point by adding Bruno's behaviour last night is an example. "Let's go to Signore Murdoch's Inn."

We exchanged kisses and goodbyes. Once again I was alone, I went to the storeroom with a piece of cheese in my hand.

* * *

It was noon and I grew concerned because there was still no sign of Signora Rossi. Dark images ran through my mind. I hoped and prayed that I would hear the keys rattling but it did not happen.

In order to banish the fears and worries away, I busied myself by cleaning the café. I must have done those chores three or four times that day only to make the time pass by.

She must have gotten one of those headaches and couldn't make it so she decided to take some time off, I thought. Signora Rossi said that her husband was invited to a party, so I guessed that maybe she joined him and stayed up late, Another possible scenario was that maybe they made up and spent the day together. There were so many possibilities but the frightening fact remained that Signora Rossi did not appear. There was so many people coming to the café and leaving, asking questions, talking to each other outside the door. I could hear them clearly saying that it was unusual of her to close without leaving any note on the door. Others said that they hoped nothing serious happened to her.

Time elapsed so slowly but my worries increased by the minute. I went to the storeroom and to my surprise, it was dark. I looked at the windows and the sky was dark. I estimated that it must have been around 6 o'clock, but there very was little I could do except wait and hope that she is alright. I was so hungry. I did not have anything to eat all day so I made myself a cheese and tomato sandwich and got myself a glass of milk. I sat at the table near the door.

Just as I was about to take my third bite, heavy banging on the door almost caused me to choke on my food.

"Who's there?" I asked in trepidation.

"Open up! Is she there? Is there anyone in there?" It was Signore Rossi. I instantly recognised his voice and he seemed very irate.

"No, Signore. Signora Rossi is not here." My heart was thumping so fast that I feared it might leap out of my chest. I was afraid of him, I was always afraid of him. To my surprise, he began kicking the doors so hard and screaming,

"I always told her that I never liked that bitch!" Signore Rossi was talking about Signora Rossellini. I thought that the glass door would cave in at any minute. "Did she come in today?"

I paused for a while and did not know what to say. I wanted to say something but feared that it might put Signora Rossi in trouble.

"Answer me, answerer me!" His screaming and banging at the door made me so scared.

"No, she didn't come in today," I answered while crying.

"I'll get the spare keys and come back." At that moment I realised the enormity of the problem. I ran to the storeroom. I lit a candle and without thinking, I called Formaggio. It took only moments for him to come out and I held him in my hand while sitting on one of the boxes.

"Do you know, my friend, that Signora Rossi is in trouble? She's not here yet. It's the first time that her husband ever came to the café. I think Signora Rossellini's tips have worked and got him to react. See, Formaggio, even in a storeroom and locked behind doors, there's still no peace. If it wasn't for you, Formaggio, I wouldn't have made it this far. Thank you and I hope Signora Rossi is safe. That's all, you can go now, but I will see you later, my friend."

Shortly after my little chat with Formaggio, I heard the unmistakable sound of rattling of keys. Once again my heart pulsated furiously.

"Is that you, Signora Rossi?" I asked. Fear made my body go numb as I saw him. He was in civilian clothing as he opened the glass door. I moved back. He saw that I was distraught and my eyes were still red after crying. To my surprise, he was very cordial.

"Listen, Salem, I didn't mean to scare you. I was just worried about her. The kids are really worried," Signore Rossi explained softly.

"*Si*, I am worried, too," I said. "Do you want anything to drink?"

"No thank you, Salem. I must return home to be with Alexander and Sofia."

"Maybe she stayed the night with Signora Rossellini and over slept, or maybe she is at home by now," I said.

"It's getting late. Listen, Salem, I will go to the house. If she's not there I'll come to you." Signore Rossi patted me on the shoulder and said, "*Arrivederci*, Salem."

"*Arrivederci*, Signore Rossi. *Buona fortuna*," I replied.

With that, he turned and left, locking the café again. Although I stood there and was again alone, I felt a bit better so I sat and finished my sandwich.

It was not long before I heard the keys in the keyhole. Every part of me was filled with excitement and hope. I prayed that Signora Rossi was behind those doors ... and she was! The beautiful but tired face of Signora Rossi appeared. Once she opened the second door, I ran to her and put my hands around her.

"*Where were you*? Signora Rossi" I asked adding that I was worried about her.

"I'm so sorry to put you through this. It was so foolish of me. I was a broken woman last night. Now I'm broken and guilty," Signora Rossi said with tears in her eyes.

"Signore Rossi was here earlier on looking for you. First he was mad but then he came with a spare key and he was calm,"

I explained. "He said Alexander and Sofia are really worried about you."

Signora Rossi sighed, sat herself on the chair and lit a cigarette. She was very tired and talked a lot about the night before. Again she cried under the influence of the red wine and the effect of the emotional betrayal. Signore Rossi came to the café and he was so happy to see his wife there. He walked toward her and placed a kiss on her forehead.

"I was so worried about you. I looked for you everywhere. Are you all right?" Signore Rossi asked in a very gentle and caring voice.

"You don't care anymore! You really ignored and embarrassed me in front of my best friend. That night you made me a laughing stock in front of your friends. You really broke my heart, Bruno!" Signora Rossi sobbed and dabbed a tissue to her eyes.

"I love you with all my heart, but the pressure of my job has made me forget about myself most of the time, and that night I was so angry that you were with that fornicating woman. I really am sorry. Please forgive me. I'll make it up to you, I promise. Please come home. The children really miss you."

"I will go home, but I want you to accept that Angelica is my best friend. Also I won't leave that poor creature on his own after what we both put him through. He has to come with us," Signora Rossi demanded.

Signore Rossi submitted to his wife totally. "*Si, Allegra, amore mio*. Anything you want, just come home. The kids are probably going crazy at this stage."

Signora Rossi called me. "Salem, bring your pyjamas because you're coming with us to our home and will spend the night with Sofia and Alexander."

My heart jumped with joy, but still I looked at Signore Rossi to see his reaction. He smiled and nodded his head that I had his approval. I left a small piece of cheese for Formaggio.

Some minutes later we were outside and driving through Benghazi.

"Wow, Benghazi is really pretty at night time!" I said. I felt free and happy.

Finally we arrived at Signora Rossi's place. The reception that Signora Rossi got from the children and Signorina De Luca was better than she expected. Alexander and Sofia were so happy to see me there and they were puzzled to see me in the company of their father.

That night Signora Rossi made delicious food. We all ate together and had cheesecake for dessert. Signora Rossi asked Signorina De Luca to make a bed for me in the children's room. She too could not believe it and looked in the direction of Signore Rossi, who was drinking some wine while reading the evening paper. There was some confusion and I was sure that it was only a temporary thing. Upon leaving the apartment the following morning, however, she assured me from now on that I would be spending the entire weekend with them.

The *Orsini* docked at the port of Benghazi and there were large masses of Italian settlers dancing and waving the Italian flags, singing, "Glory to Roma, the Il Duce and General Graziani." Meanwhile Sidi Omar was walking slowly as the heavy chains around his wrists and ankles were cumbersome. Despite his age, Sidi Omar walked like a wounded lion.

General Graziani had just arrived and gave orders that Al-Mukhtar had to be prosecuted in a military court with immediate effect. Sidi Omar's fate was decided long ago, long before his capture. Sidi Omar was tried, found guilty and sentenced to death by hanging. But worst of all, he was to be hanged in front of his people – the prisoners in the concentration camps. This was a powerful example of Graziani's ruthless mind and arrogance to inflict pain upon the already humiliated and broken people.

* * *

On the evening of 15 September, General Graziani asked his officers to bring Al-Mukhtar to his office in an attempt to further humiliate and degrade the man who had been a thorn in Rome's side since their landing on the shores of Benghazyi twenty years earlier.

That evening, General Graziani was sitting behind his desk in the Italian Military Headquarters in Benghazi. He was studying some reports, and on the wall behind him was a huge poster of Il Duce, Benito Mussolini. Graziani was in full military uniform. After a few minutes, an officer knocked on his door.

"*Entrare*," he said and two soldiers entered the office escorting Sidi Omar. They saluted the general and then they left Sidi Omar standing in the middle of the room. Before exiting, they shut the door. Sidi Omar was chained. General Graziani did not steer his eyes away from the reports. He purposefully ignored Al-Mukhtar's presence for few minutes and then he threw his pencil on the desk, stood up and fixed his jacket. He stared at Sidi Omar, but he was startled upon gazing at the old man and he was not able to conceal it. Graziani had not expected to see an old man before him as the general had never seen Al-Mukhtar prior to this.

"Omar, finally you're at our mercy," Graziani said with pride, and then opened the drawer in his desk and took out Sidi Omar's spectacles. "When they brought me your glasses, I knew you weren't far behind." Then he handed him the glasses.

"*Grazie*, General. Our fate was written before we were born and I don't regret one single moment of my life."

"Why did you fight us all this time when you really knew that you had no hope in hell in defeating us?"

"Because it's our duty to defend our country and it's our cause to strive against the invader," Sidi Omar replied while he was lifting the chains with his hands to relieve some of the load straining his frail body. Graziani was not oblivious to Omar's discomfort but did not offer Al-Mukhtar a chair, instead preferring to watch the man endure more pain.

"You're fighting for Alsonussi. Isn't that right, Omar?" the general asked while he was walking around the office with his hands behind his back.

"You're totally wrong, General; we fight for our country. We fight because it's our duty to defend and die for our country. We don't fight for the glory of others."

"How long do you think it will take for the rebels to lay down their arms?"

"This is will never happen, General. There will be new generations, new blood, they will fight you until they see the back of the last soldier leaving this country," Sidi Omar responded.

"Don't you think you're ruining your country by fighting us?"

"You are the ruination of my country. No nation has the right to occupy another. We will never surrender. We win or we die. As for me, I will live longer than my hangman."

Graziani had heard a lot about Al-Mukhtar from his predecessors, about how brave and unbreakable he was. Graziani never imagined that Omar was this strongwilled, even in the face of his own death.

Graziani looked at Al-Mukhtar with respect, and then he put on his cap.

"Before I leave," Sidi Omar said, "I ask of you only one favour."

Graziani nodded his head once. "What is it, Omar?"

"Please don't tell the world any lies about our meeting behind these closed doors."

"You have got that, Omar. I promise." Then he called the guards to come and take Al-Mukhtar to his cell. Graziani followed Sidi Omar with his eyes until the door closed. Graziani later wrote in his memoirs that Omar Al-Mukhtar was a man of honour and integrity. A man who loved his religion and his country, never accepted any bribes from the Italian Government and never submitted to their will.

On the morning of 16 September 1931, Sidi Omar was brought out from his prison cell and escorted by heavily armed guards. There were a huge number of people from the Italian media, the local people, and the Italian community in Benghazi. He was chained but he looked so calm and was cordial to all of those who wanted to take a picture with him. Then he was put in a military car heading for the village of Slooq by the orders of Graziani, to be hanged in front of thousands of people of the Green Mountain who were brought from the concentration camps.

Upon the car's arrival, there were thousands of people looking miserable and desperate. These prisoners were guarded by hundreds of Italian soldiers and Ariterean mercenaries, to crush any revolt by the people. Sidi Omar was escorted and helped up the steps to the gallows and was placed under the noose. While the soldiers began to release him from the chains, he gazed down at the people who supported him during the struggle. He looked deep into their eyes and they were full of tears. Sidi Omar was so calm and kept smiling, especially to the young children. He seemed so content, like a man that could see his fate in the hereafter.

Soon the executioner took Sidi Omar's spectacles, tightened his hands behind his back and placed the noose around the man's neck. A deadly silence befell the people and Omar's executioner awaited the order to proceed from the officer in charge.

At that time, the people who stood near the gallows could hear Sidi Omar reciting from the Quran. "Oh, thou soul, complete rest and satisfaction! Come back thou to thy Lord, well pleased thyself and well pleasing unto him. Enter thou then, among my devotees. Yes, enter thou my heavens!"

Then the executioner received the sign from the officer by a nodding of the officer's–head. A trapdoor was opened from underneath Sidi Omar's feet and his body dropped. His followers' hearts dropped also.

The customers were in a curious mood and they wanted to know what happened the day before and why the café was closed. Signora Rossi and I gave them no answers. By 4 o'clock the café was full to the brim and everyone carried newspapers.

Many customers were shouting, arguing and celebrating because the military court had sentenced Omar Al-Mukhtar to death by hanging. The verdict was ordered by General Graziani and granted by the general governor of Libya before the trial even began. Documents, which were discovered after the Second World War, later proved that the trial was a farce.

Signora Rossi and I coped well with the pressure. We did not talk much but kept smiling at each other. She wore a look of sadness on her face and we never spoke about what happened the previous night. Daowud looked so restless and he was looking behind him every time someone came to the café. I think he was waiting for Signora Rossellini to appear but she never made it that day.

We closed later than usual that evening as the celebrations went on and Fat Toni was unable to resist the opportunity to revel in Omar Al-Mukhtar's death. He took his newspaper, stood up with one hand holding his glass and with the other he was waving the paper in the air. With that, all hell broke loose. I always enjoyed those arguments and quarrels between Fat Toni and the Libyan crowd. It was fun and made the day pass quicker.

By the time we finished it was late, but Signora Rossi said that it was another successful day. She did not hang on there for long . Signora Rossi went home and I stayed in the shop. I was so tired from the previous few days, which were emotional and eventful.

The next morning we had to open an hour earlier because some extra cleaning had to be done before the café could open for business. We could not finish all the cleaning and the setting up the night before. Once all this was completed, Signora Rossi began making a big list of all the things we needed as we were low in stock. The café was very quiet as was expected because many people went to witness the execution of Sidi Omar. Others decided to stay in their homes in case of any revolt by the locals.

"Salem, I think I'll take advantage of the situation and go to the wholesale to give them the list, hoping that they will deliver the next day," Signora Rossi said while taking off her apron.

"Si, I will manage on my own. I don't think it will be busy," I replied.

"I won't be long, Salem, I promise," Signora Rossi assured me. After Signora Rossi left, only couple of people came in and I managed very well. When she returned she was very proud of me for not panicking.

"You can start taking time off from now on because the boy is very good," one customer said.

In the afternoon, Signore Rossi walked in full uniform. "*Buongiorno*," he greeted us.

"Buongiorno, Signore Rossi," I replied, feeling uncomfortable about the unusual and unexpected visit.

"Wow, what a surprise! Which wind has sent you to our direction?" Signora Rossi asked with a big smile on her face.

"I'm just back from the military headquarters. Omar Al-Mukhtar has been executed and there was no revolt or unrest among the prisoners of the concentration camps who witnessed the execution." Signore Rossi took off his cap and kissed Signora Rossi on the lips. "I won't be home for dinner because I have to attend a late meeting. *Ciao, Arrivaderci*," Signore Rossi confirmed before making his way to the door.

"*Ciao, buona fortuna, mio amore*," she replied.

That night I did not have much sleep as Signore Rossi's unexpected visit to the café made me think and my mind was filled with unpleasant thoughts, but I did not know why. Only the late appearance of Formaggio changed my mood and made those unwelcomed thoughts vanish. If he had not, then it would have been a long night devoid of any sleep.

CHAPTER SEVENTEEN

Christmas was only few days away and there was a feeling of excitement around the whole Piazza. A big tree in the middle of it was decorated with so many different coloured fairy lights.

Signora Rossi and Signora Rossellini constantly told me that we had to live the spirit of Christmas so they decorated the café and it was very colourful. We were very busy both day and night, as the Italian settlers were coming from everywhere around the countryside to do their shopping and buy presents. The shops opened all week for the last fortnight so Signora Rossi took her children and myself, she bought us new good quality clothes. She also took us for lunch in a luxurious hotel.

Thankfully, the weather changed in Benghazi and there was not much rain, but the skies were dull most of the time. The last few months had given me good idea of what was happening in my country as Dawoud, Najeeb and Faouzi started answering all my questions. They also gave me the newspaper to read and informed me that the concentration camps were still there and the situation in Al-agaila was worsening by the day. Later I was told that Sidi Omar's men started putting their arms down and negotiated a peace treaty to guarantee their safety and avoid any punishment from the Italian government in Cyrenaica.

Signora Rossellini and her affair with Dawoud was no longer a secret as Fat Toni Maltese, notoriously known for his big mouth, let it slip one evening in the café. Even the denial from Dawoud and the intervention of Signora Rossi in an attempt to protect her best friend's reputation, did not stop Fat Toni.

"Toni knows everything in the Square," was his reply. This was his answer to everything. Normally nobody took Toni seriously but Signora Rossi threatened him that if he continued his rumours, she would boycott his shop and never buy her meat from him again.

"Can't a guy joke in this town or what?" he replied wittily and everybody got a kick out of it. Toni was a character, funny and well liked. Despite his love for gossip, he always added some spice to the atmosphere in the café. Many of Signora Rossi's friends dropped by and had a little chat before she asked them to call in tomorrow for a glass of wine.

When we finished that day, Signora Rossi and I sat down for a little rest.

"Toni was very funny today, wasn't he, Signora Rossi?" I said.

"*Sì*, he's very funny and I do like him, but his big mouth can land him in trouble sometimes," Signora Rossi answered while trying to ease the tension in her neck by twisting her head left and right. "It's been good, Salem, since your arrival. It's been a good six months and I believe that you've brought me some sort of luck."

"*Grazie mille*, and you've been like a mother to me, and if it wasn't for you, I don't know what would've happened to me in Al-agaila. Thanks for helping me."

"Okay, little man, this is the deal. Tomorrow is Christmas Eve, and as a custom, I have always opened for a half day for my loyal customers to show them my appreciation for their support. So I give them couple of glasses each so it's more like a socialising event rather than business," Signora Rossi explained.

"That's very nice of you," I responded.

"*Grazie*. So, I want you to put all your clothes and your pillow cases and quilt cover all in your bag tomorrow morning and have it ready," Signora Rossi said.

I got scared and immediately asked, "Is it to do with Signore Rossi's visit the other day? Am I going back there? Please tell me Signora Rossi I will work harder. I'll stay in the storeroom. I will–"

"Salem, calm down." Signora Rossi put her arms around me and held me tight. She saw the tears in my eyes and cried, "Oh, my poor baby, is that why you were so quiet last night? It's the opposite, my sweetheart. You'll be spending the Festive holiday with us. We will close the shop for three days. Don't ever think that I'll send you back to that horrible place. Come, smile. Show me your beautiful smile." Signora Rossi smoothed down my hair and wiped away my tears.

The next day was more like a family get-together. Most people were standing in circles chatting to each other. Signora Rossi was going around with the wine for a refill. I was going around with cheese and little snacks, which were prepared earlier on by Signora Rossi. Every costumer we knew was there. Fat Toni was the main attraction as he was moving from one circle to another, sniffing for more gossip and spreading it at the same time. All Signora Rossi's female friends were present and Signora Rossellini was glamorous as always. Daowud was trying his best not to make any form of eye contact with her as he was probably warned not to. He knew that he could not afford to give Fat Toni any excuses. He managed, however, to elicit a wink or a smile from time to time. Soon people were requesting for someone to sing and to everyone's surprise, Fat Toni was the star of the afternoon. Toni sang love songs and carols. He was superb and possessed a fantastic voice.

Closing time soon arrived and everyone thanked Signora Rossi and me for a lovely afternoon. I got a lot of money from the customers that day and most of it came from Fat Toni and the Libyan crowd. I gave it all to Signora Rossi and she said that she would save for me. Only some of Signora Rossi's friends had remained at 2 o'clock and they helped in getting the café in order. While the ladies were making arrangements for Christmas night, I snuck to the storeroom and left Formaggio a piece of cheese. We closed the shop and we exchanged greetings with her friends and made our way home.

Sofia and Alexander were already there as they had finished school early. They were so delighted to see me and they were jumping with joy when they learned from their mother that

I would be spending a few days with them. Signora Rossi immediately tied her apron around her waist and busied herself in the kitchen with Signorina De Luca, preparing food and sweets for "the big day" as Signora Rossi described it. The house was magnificently decorated and was like walking into a magical wonderland.

That evening Signore Rossi put on very soothing background music. He lit his pipe and started wrapping presents for his family. Sofia and Alexander did the same and they explained everything to me about the occasion. In the corner of the sitting room stood a splendid Christmas tree which was expertly decorated. Lots of presents were placed underneath it. Signora Rossi and Signorina De Luca were still stuck in the kitchen preparing everything from cooking the turkey to making the perfect sauces. Both women never forgot about us, as they emerged a number of times with drinks and cakes.

After couple of hours, Signora Rossi called everybody for a light snack. We ate but did not stay up for long as she wanted us to get good night sleep and be up early for mass and be energetic for Christmas Day. Signora Rossi slipped into something comfortable after a quick wash and joined her husband for a drink. Signorina De Luca took us up to bed and told us a tale about heroes and their endless adventures. The soft December rain pounded the windowpane, which added an extra element of mystique to the bedtime story. Early in the morning we were up and Signorina De Luca assisted the children in getting dressed for church.

"That's what we do first," explained Sofia.

"Then when we come back, we open the presents," Alexander added. "I can't wait."

I put on my new clothes that Signora Rossi got me a week earlier. There was a real exciting atmosphere around the place. Signora and Signore Rossi were already up, fully dressed and having their morning coffee. They looked elegant. Signora Rossi made us light breakfast, then we were all ready.

"You will wait here for us Salem. We won't be long, it's only an hour and we'll all be here. Is that okay?"

"Si, Signora Rossi, I'll be fine." They all went and if I am to be honest, I felt unwanted and could not understand Signora Rossi's actions. However, all these miserable feelings evaporated upon the family's return after Signora Rossi saw how withdrawn I had become. She took me to the room, put her arms on my shoulder and said,

"Listen, Salem, I know you're upset and it's normal to feel that way because you t,hought you weren't welcome to come with us but I was doing that for you, do you understand?"

"No, Signora Rossi I don't understand!"

"Salem, you're a Muslim, and I didn't want to influence your faith. I made that promise from the time we took you out of that horrible place. That's the reason we didn't take you with us to the church. Do you understand now?" Signora Rossi's eyes met mine as if she wanted to see that I fully understood her actions. I hugged her and told her again how wonderful she was and how much she meant to me.

There were screams of excitement from Alexander and Sofia as they set upon the presents under the Christmas tree. Everyone got what they wanted and once the opening of the presents was over, kisses and hugs were exchanged around the room. I got the vast majority of the gifts and everyone, even Signore Rossi, had something for me. Most of my presents were good clothes and Italian books. I was so delighted and felt that I was part of this good family. I was happy and thanked them all.

It took couple of hours for things to calm down. Then the two ladies were confined to the kitchen once again. We took our presents up to Sofia and Alexander's room and studied them in detail.

The day passed slowly and music played all day in the background. By 4 o'clock, the dinner table was dressed and it looked immaculate. Everything was shining. At that particular time, Signore Rossi went to a cabinet and took out few bottles of wine. He opened the bottles and placed them on the table. Signorina De Luca was placing the vegetables dishes on the table. Then Signora Rossi came with the turkey; it was on a silver plate and looked so delicious. Soon Signora Rossi made the call for everyone to take a seat at the dinner table. There was total silence and after Signore Rossi said grace, we all began eating. He sliced the turkey and gave everyone a sizable portion. The vegetable dishes passed around and Signora Rossi was filling Signore Rossi and Signorina De Luca's glasses with wine. There was not much talking except for the compliments that were passed from time to time to both ladies for their excellent food.

Italians really love their food and wine, and to them it is like a religion, for the Italians cocking is like a religious ritual. Signora Rossi spoke about the good year she was having and how the business was thriving. She did not forget to praise me for my hard work.

"Salem has brought luck with him to the place and he is a very good worker."

Then my mind drifted back to that miserable Christmas time in Al-agaila when we had to eat hot water with feathers as a soup and we were told that was a treat from the soldiers. It was horrid. What I was eating at Signore Rossi's house *was* food and undoubtedly *was* a treat. After dinner came dessert and it was so divine!

Once we stuffed ourselves, we did help the ladies clear the table. Then everyone moved slowly to find a comfortable seat, or even a bed. We did nap for about an hour or so. When we woke up, the place was clean and the table was set once again and we all started getting dressed again as Signora Rossi said it was a custom for us to receive friends on the evening of this day and warned us to be on our best behaviour. I was delighted to hear that there would be few children coming.

One by one the Rossi's guests start arriving along with their children. Signora Rossellini was one of the guests and her husband came too. Signore Rossi surprised me by welcoming her warmly and did not seem to hold any grudge against her. The adults mingled with each other and so did the children. We went up to Alexander's room and I told everyone about Formaggio. Of course, I couldn't tell them that he was a real mouse because that would cause some concern for Signora Rossi, and maybe have him killed. Instead, I told them that he was a ghost and how I learned to cope with him being in the room alone by night. The children believed me and I chuckled as they were more than a little spooked by my tale.

The party continued for a quite a while before the guests left just before midnight. Signore Rossellini invited everybody to his house for the New Year's party and it was another great night.

Signora Rossi took us out for a walk by the beach the next day and we visited few people. All the ladies organised a picnic for all the children on the third day and we went to the forest in the outskirts of Benghazi. It was a brilliant day. We played so many games and had lots of fun. Those few days of Christmas and the New Year were the most enjoyable days of my life because I felt like a child. I felt human. I continued spending the weekends with the Rossi's and I was invited to every occasion. Despite all the fun I had, I did miss Formaggio and he missed me, too I believe.

After the New Year's celebrations, nothing much happened except that more Italians immigrants have arrived to Cyrenaica, after learning that Omar Al-Mukhtar was dead and his men had laid down their arms after reaching an agreement with the Italian Government in Libya that would give them immunity and spare their lives. The days went by and became weeks and the weeks became months, and it was in March of 1932 when Signora Rossi comforted me after finishing work.

"Sit down, Salem, I really need to talk to you. Please don't take what I'm about to say to you in the wrong way. *Capisce?*" Signora Rossi asked.

"*Si, capisco.*"

"It's very hard for me, Salem, but it's not fair to keep you away from your loved ones. Do you know that after the return of Omar's men from their camps, they started making enquiries about their families in the concentration camps and their fate. Someone had requested information about your family. Do you know any relations that may still alive?"

"*Si*, my uncle," I replied.

"Well he did ask and he was told of their fate, but he was also told that a young child called Salem was still alive and that he was safe and being taken care of by an Italian family in Benghazi. The officers there have informed my husband and now they're in the process of finding him." Signora Rossi paused and then explained that I might have to depart from them when my uncle come for me, it's for your best interest Salem, she added. Tears ran down my cheeks. Signora Rossi took me into her arms and said, "That could take weeks or even months. So don't be hard on yourself, my boy."

I buried my head in her bosoms and sobbed like a baby. "I will miss you, Signora Rossi. I will miss Sofia and Alexander and will miss the café and the customers. I'll miss Benghazi." I cried in her arms and never wanted to let her go. Signora Rossi wiped my tears.

"Come on, show me that beautiful smile of yours," she said. I smiled, but I was saddened by the fact that I would soon be losing her, but also happy that my uncle was still alive and was looking for me. I must say that I missed home and missed my friends in the mountain. I also missed my dog, Saiyad.

Signora Rossi and I continued to work so hard and she took every opportunity to make me happier, and every time she noticed that I was feeling down, she used to take me home with her.

The days went by and my heart was torn. I bonded more with Signora Rossi than ever before. In those two years, I had grown up quickly but there was more for me to learn.

I learned that the spirit can triumph and rise from the wreckage when one possesses love and faith.

CHAPTER EIGHTEEN

Finally the news arrived when Signore Rossi made an unexpected visit to the café one afternoon at the end of the sunny month of May 1932. He was in full uniform, and the minute he entered the café he took off his cap and greeted everyone present.

"*Buongiorno, Allegra. Buongiorno, Salem,*" Then he went behind the counter and kissed Signora Rossi on the cheek.

"Is everything all right, darling?" Signora Rossi asked.

"Yes, nothing to worry about," he replied. "I have good news for Salem. We have located his uncle!" Signore Rossi explained while his eyes were fixed on me.

"How is he? Is he all right? Does he know that I'm alive?" I asked him, feeling so happy that he was back safe from his camp. Signora Rossi explained everything to me about Sidi Omar's men who finally laid down their arms after his death.

"Yes, Salem, he's in good form and was very delighted to hear that you have been looked after. He was also informed about the rest of your family members. I was told that he was devastated." There was an amalgamation of concern and sincerity in Signore Rossi's voice.

"He was my mother's only brother. He is very kind man. I missed him," I added with tears on the brink of rolling over the ducts so I turned and went to the storeroom. In there, I let my tears run freely.

Signora Rossi followed me and said, "It will be good for you to be with your loved ones. And Salem, I'll always be here if you ever need me."

Once we returned to the front room, Signore Rossi delivered the news that my uncle was coming to collect me in two weeks. "I have arranged for him to come with the military post vehicle that comes here from the Green Mountain every second week and you will be getting a lift back home in the same car as it leaves few hours later."

So that was it. Yet again I had to depart from someone I truly loved. Signora Rossi walked her husband out after the goodbyes. They talked for a few minutes before she returned.

"Wow, two weeks. That's only a fortnight, and then we have to say goodbye, Salem. We have to make the best out of what's left. You will spend the whole two weeks with us, Salem. We will do so many things together and will visit many places. I'll have the best party for you, Salem, to give you the best send-off." Signora Rossi spoke so enthusiastically and was like a child. But the truth behind it was that Signora Rossi hid the pain that she felt. Despite us both wanting every minute to last a lifetime, everything must come to an end.

Signora Rossi hung a small note on the door saying "Worker wanted", and it was only a couple of days before this attractive girl walked in and introduced herself as Signorina Maria Brenaizi. We both liked her, and by the next morning Signora Rossi and I were helping her to familiarise herself with the place.

"I think she's going to be great. She's smart and pretty and people like her," I said to assure her that everything would be fine.

"No one can fill the gap that you're going to leave behind, Salem, but yes, she's good and I liked her from the moment she walked into the place and that's very important," Signora Rossi replied.

All the customers were very saddened upon hearing about my departure. Everyone offered words of encouragement and wished me the best of luck. Out of all of them, however, Fat Toni was the most affected by the news and he made a collection for me. I gave the money to Signora Rossi. She always said that she would give back the money that I earned when the time is right. Signora Rossi fulfilled her promise and took me everywhere with her, and a few days before leaving she invited all the children to her place to say goodbye. It was emotional.

Sofia cried and told me that she would never forget me.

On Wednesday evening, just one day before my departure from the Rossi family and at the dinner table, Signora Rossi spoke gently to her children.

"Listen, and listen very carefully. I know how upset you are but you must know that Salem is going to be with his family and he will be in the place where he was born, among his people, and that's very important for everyone. There's no place like home, so I want you to wish him well and pray for him. Do you understand?"

"Si, Mama, but can't Salem stay? His uncle can come and visit him whenever he wants," Alexander replied.

"Listen, son, people are like birds, and no matter how long and far they fly away, eventually they will come back to their nests and that's home. We, too, have to go home some day."

Sofia frowned and said, "But this is our home. We were born here."

Signora Rossi paused for a few seconds and looked at her husband for some assistance.

"*Si*, you have a point, Sofia. This is your home and yes you were born here, but your mum and I came here from Italy and once I have finished my service, I, too, want to go home," Signore Rossi added. Signora Rossi sighed with relief. Alexander and Sofia looked at each other and eventually accepted the fact that I was going and there was nothing that they could do except spend that night talking about the good year we had together.

Once dinner was devoured, we helped Signora Rossi with the dishes and cleared the table. She made us hot milk and gave us slices of cake. Signore Rossi confined himself to his favourite seat, lit up his pipe and waited for the coffee that his wife made him after dinner. He kept looking at me all night, and every time I met his eyes he smiled and nodded his head up and down. In other words, he was trying to say that I would be okay.

Signora Rossi began organising my two suitcases, large one and a small one. There was so much stuff that I had collected over the year. So many clothes, presents and books. I saw Signora Rossi crying while putting my things in the cases. That night Signora Rossellini came to say goodbye and brought me a good present. She paid me a lot of compliments and encouraged me to do well in life. That was the last time I saw her. Alexander, Sofia and I stayed up most of the night talking about the good and bad memories of the year, and my friendly ghost, Formaggio.

In the morning, Signore Rossi wore his uniform and was sipping his coffee. Signorina De Luca got the children ready for school. It was only few weeks before they finished for the summer holidays. Signora Rossi packed their lunch boxes.

Then came the moment that I hated the most: saying goodbye to Alexander and Sofia.

"Come on, children, time to wish Salem good luck," Signora Rossi said, trying to avoid the word "goodbye". Alexander came forward and gave me his favourite toy.

"No, Alexander, I couldn't take it. It's your favourite," I insisted.

"But I want you to remember me with it," Alexander cried.

"I don't need the toy to remember you, Alexander. I will remember you all my life. Please keep it so you will remember me more," I said before hugging him.

Then Sofia handed me a book. "You'll like it, Salem. It's about a brave boy who lost his family but he makes it home in the end."

"*Grazie*, Sofia." I took her in my arms.

Signorina De Luca kissed my forehead and said, "You're a good boy and you'll have no problem making it in this life."

Then Sofia, Alexander and Signorina De Luca headed for the door. Before the door closed behind them, I heard Sofia saying to Alexander that the house would be empty without me.

Signore Rossi put his cap on, kissed Signora Rossi and told her, "Bring him to the headquarters by noon." Then he turned to me and said, "I shall see you in few hours, kid."

Signora Rossi prepared the bath for me and took out the best clothes to wear. She wanted me to look my best when meeting my uncle. She too got dressed and, as always, looked smashing.

It finally came time for me to leave. Signora Rossi put the suitcases by the door and asked me to come with her. She sat me on the edge of the bed and knelt down on one knee.

"Salem, this is the moment that I've always feared, that I dreaded to face, but I knew one day you would depart from me.

I grieve because you're leaving me, but I'm also celebrating the fact that you will be with one of your own. I know he will make you happy. You're the only one left for him and he is the only one left for you. Salem, embrace this opportunity and cherish every minute with him. You're a special boy, I knew that from the moment I saw you in Al-agaila, and you will do well in life because despite what happened to you and what you had to go through, you still have plenty of love in your heart and I'm so sorry for every minute that you had to sleep on your own in the storeroom. I have suffered for you, but I can't forgive myself, so please forgive me." Signora Rossi wept like a baby while holding my hands tightly. I wiped her tears away with my fingers.

"I, too, have suffered for all the trouble you went through for me. Thank you for such a great year. You were like a mother to me and I really do appreciate that."

"Salem, make a promise to me,? Promise to come see me if you're near here."

"I will. I promise."

"Okay, it's time, Salem. We have to go. Come on, darling."

"Si," I replied, while standing at the edge of the bed. I gave one last glance around the place that contained some of my best childhood memories. We picked up the suitcases and closed the door behind us. Signora Rossi held my hand while carrying the suitcase. I was carrying the small one but there was not much walking to be done.

Lots of thoughts were swimming around my head such as the excitement of seeing Uncle Saleh and going home to see my friends and my dog. Of course, there was also the sadness of leaving Signora Rossi and Benghazi.

"Signora Rossi, could you do me a big favour, please?" I asked.

"Si, Salem, anything you want, just ask."

"Can we pass by the café? I would like to spend a minute or two on my own there."

"Si. Anything for you, my boy." The café was closed that day as Signora Rossi put a sign up the night before stating that it would be closed Thursday and would reopen on Friday. Once we arrived there, Signora Rossi opened the two doors and said, "I will wait outside."

I walked slowly to the counter and took a small piece of cheese before I went to the storeroom. "Formaggio, where are you? Come to me, my good friend."

Formaggio came out very quickly and ran onto my palm. I put him close to my face.

"Listen, my friend, I want to say thank you and tell you how much I owe you for making staying on my own bearable. I couldn't have done it without you, but I also came to tell you that I'm leaving for good and we may never be able to see each other again. So, farewell, my good friend and be extra vigilant as the next person may not be as kind."

I kissed him and put him down on the floor. I gave him the piece of cheese, but before he touched it, he looked at me with his small but deep black eyes. To me, and as strange as this may sound, it felt as if he was telling me to look after myself and that he would be fine. That was the last time I saw Formaggio, but that little mouse lived with me forever, as he was the hero in the bedtime stories for my little children. I thanked Signora Rossi before we closed up the café and headed for the military camp where Signore Rossi was based.

At the gate a soldier greeted Signora Rossi. "*Buongiorno*, Signora Rossi. You're looking very well. Your husband is waiting for you. Please come in."

"*Grazie mille*, you're very kind," Signora Rossi replied with a big smile as she acknowledged the compliment. We walked towards Signore Rossi's office.

"That's the office there on the first floor of that building." Signora Rossi indicated by pointing to it with her left hand.

As one would expect, there was lots of activity in the camp. All sorts of military cars were arriving and departing. Soldiers were marching and training. Signora Rossi took me by the hand once again when we approached the office. We saw Signore Rossi standing by the window and he stared at us. When we were standing directly below the entrance to the building containing his office, he came out to us.

"*Buongiorno*, darling. *Buongiorno*, Salem," Signore Rossi greeted us. We greeted him back and then he spoke softly to me. "Listen, Salem, your Uncle Saleh is here now in my office. He has been informed of everything. He knows that you're going to be here and he knows that he's taking you with him. I just want to tell you that I am sorry for what happened to you. I think you are very special boy and you will successor in whatever you choose to do in life."

To be honest, I was shocked by what Signore Rossi had said. Never in my wildest dreams did I imagine him heaping all this praise on me. He then placed his hand on my shoulder and continued,

"I will let him know you're outside. Farewell, Salem." That was the last time I saw Signore Rossi, and for years I was trying to find an answer or maybe a good reason for him not accepting me, especially at the very beginning. Was it because of the extra attention I was receiving from Signora Rossi? Or was it because to him; I served as a constant reminder of the brutality of the concentration camp and that he did not want to be reminded of that? I never really did find out but his words to me that afternoon showed that he had some respect for me.

Signora Rossi and I were standing in the shade of a huge tree when my Uncle Saleh appeared. He was looking everywhere and looked at us twice but turned his head in other directions as he did not recognise me. Uncle Saleh was looking for the same kid he saw more than two years ago. I was looking more Italian with the way I was dressed. He did not change much, but was still as tall as ever and a bit skinnier. His hair was very long and he had a long beard. When I saw him, I shouted his name with an amalgamation of delight and sorrow. We ran to each other and he got on his knees to give me a big hug. He started weeping and then pushed me back gently to look at my face and then hugged me again. He repeated this few times and we both cried while Signora Rossi wiped the tears away from her eyes. From looking at Signore Rossi at his office window, I could tell that even he looked like he was touched by our reunion.

"You've turned into a fine looking boy!" my uncle said while he was wiping his tears with his handkerchief. "You look like you have been looked after so well."

"Yes, and I would like you to meet the lady who took me out of the camp and looked after me for the whole year." I took him by the hand and led him toward Signora Rossi. "Uncle, this is Signora Rossi. Signora Rossi, this is my Uncle Saleh. He's my mother's only brother."

"Thank you so much for looking after him," Saleh said while shaking her hand. "It shows that he has bees looked after very well" its pleasure meeting you. My uncle added.

"The pleasure was all mine." Signora Rossi replied. She then looked at me with a motherly stare. "Salem is very special boy and I'm glad to have been part of his life. He was a pleasure to look after." Then Signora Rossi said, while trying to hide her tears, "Salem, this the moment that I've always dreaded facing, but it's our fate. Salem, I want you to know that I had the sweetest time with you and will cherish those beautiful memories forever. Just remember that promise that if you ever make it near where I live anywhere in the world, you must come and see me. I know now that you're in good hands. Go and live your life the way your mother and father wanted you to live it." After she had said this, Signora Rossi handed me an envelope full of money in the form of a bundle of notes.

"I can't take this, Signora Rossi. You've done more than enough for me."

"No, Salem, take it please. It's not a gift but the money you earned from working in the café. I will keep the rest for you until the right moment comes."

"Grazie, Signora Rossi." I handed the money to my uncle.

"I'll pray for you every day." She held me in a tight embrace. "So long, my little boy," she whispered into my ear while sobbing.

"So long, my friend," I replied.

The military post vehicle pulled up outside the building and one soldier got out of the car. He greeted us and then took the suitcases, loading them onto the back of the vehicle. Uncle

Saleh lifted me up into the back and climbed up afterwards. The soldier waved to Signore Rossi, who was still in his office, now smoking his pipe.

"Don't worry, Signora Rossi, they'll be fine," the soldier said. "I'll make sure that they make it home safe."

My uncle sat at the very front on the long wooden seat. I sat on the car floor holding onto the half door as the car was not sealed in the back. The car started moving very slowly toward the gate and Signora Rossi began following it. I was looking at her and my eyes did not leave her once. She was still following us, but the farther we drove the more she was unable to keep up. In the distance and through watery eyes, I saw her waving goodbye to me. As the gate opened, the car turned to the right and Signora Rossi vanished from my sight but never from my heart and mind.

* * *

True to my word, I did come looking for her in 1937. I was in my teens and was tall like my uncle and my father, with a slim build and a head full of curly hair. I asked my uncle to give me some of that money that Signora Rossi gave me. I told him that I will go and try my luck in Benghazi in getting a job to help him and his young family as we were struggling to make ends meet. I loved Benghazi and I knew I would come back to the city that adopted me. I had some money to keep me going for few days until I got a job. My Italian was perfect and I knew people there. My uncle, despite hating the idea that I had to leave, blessed me and asked me to come back if things did not work out.

1937 was the same year that Mussollini decided to come to Libya for his first visit bringing with him tens of thousands of new Italian settlers after the pacification of the resistance. On that day, I just made it to Benghazi. The city was decorated and was thronging with thousands of people. Thousands of soldiers and schoolchildren were amongst the vast crowd in attendance. The city was well prepared and I did go to the centre of the city where he was to give a speech. I did not go there to enjoy the day or to enjoy the buzz that the city had created for the occasion. No, I went there to spit on the man and his generals that caused so much pain for a small, peaceful nation. And I did so without making a scene. I did not even stay to listen to his very short speech that locals found meaningless and insulting.

I made my way to Signora Rossi's café. Benghazi had gotten bigger and new buildings had been built since my departure five years earlier. To my disappointment, Signora Rossi's café was gone. A tobacco shop was now in its place.

"Excuse me, signore. Did you know the lady who used to own the café here? Do you know where she's gone?" I asked the person who looked after the place.

"No, signore. This place has gone through so many owners over the last few years. Besides, I'm new to this city," he answered. Knowing that he would be of no assistance in my search for Signora Rossi, I went straight to the apartment. New people lived there too and were not able to help me either.

Signora Rossellini! I thought. Yes I should pay a visit to her. She'll be delighted to see me and help locate Signora Rossi. Or so I thought, but yet again it was another disappointment. This was too many in one day. Much like the Rossi family, there was no sign of Signora Rossellini as well.

Feeling depressed, I walked through the very busy and well-decorated streets. Everything looked so clean and new. Then the image of Fat Toni entered my head and I knew that I could go to him. If there was anybody that could help, it would be him. Plus he might pull a few strings to help me get a job and a place to stay.

Finally I got lucky. As I stood outside Fat Toni's butcher shop, I saw him there. I was so excited to go and see him. But I was not sure if he would recognise me. I fixed my jacket and walked straight up to the counter. He was cutting some meat.

"*Buongiorno, signore.*"

"*Buongiorno.* Can I help you?"

"*Si, signore.* I am looking for a lady called Signora Rossi." As soon as I had finished asking that question, he stopped what he was doing and looked at me. Then he studied me from top to bottom.

"I am sorry, kid, I don't know anyone with that name," he answered and returned to cutting the meat.

"Sure you do. Allegra Rossi, she used to own the café not far from your shop, signore." I was kind of playing games with Fat Toni.

"Who's asking?" He regarded me rather suspiciously.

"It's me, don't you remember? I used to serve you in Signora Rossi's café five years ago."

Fat Toni continued to study me until his eyes widened with glee and a look of recognition flashed across his face. "Salem, the little Libyan waiter. I can't believe what I see!" he screamed and then wiped his hands on his apron. Toni came running out from behind the counter.

"Look at you, you turned into a fine looking young man! Come here, boy." Signore Maltese hugged me and pulled up couple of chairs. "Sit down. We all missed you, Salem. Things aren't the same now. A lot of people have left. We miss the place. It used to be a great joint and it's gone now along with Signora Rossi." Signore Maltese gazed at the floor with such sad eyes for a moment before staring at me again with a smile. "How are you, son? What have you been up to?"

"I am okay. I have been living with my uncle in the Green Mountain."

Signore Maltese continued to quiz me about the last five years of my life. "So what brings you to Benghazi?"

"Well, it's a long story, but to make it short, I am here looking for a job. Things are very bad for us there, that's why I came hoping to find Signora Rossi and that maybe she can help me with a job and a place to stay."

"Don't worry, Salem, I'll help you out. You are a great kid. You've had it tough. We all liked you, Salem." Signore Maltese's answer brought some sort of relief.

"*Grazie, mille*, Signore Maltese."

"Listen, Salem, Signora Rossi left Libya in 1935. She took the kids and left to her beloved Milano. She is doing very well for herself and lives in the countryside. Signore Rossi was promoted to general and got transferred to Tripoli, but Signora Rossi never wanted to go anywhere else so she saw this as an opportunity to go back home. Signora Rossellini moved to Tripoli with her husband and you know what, Salem? That rat Dawoud vanished at the same time. That's proof of my theory about their affair. I knew it all along!" Fat Toni chatted with me for hours and was really glad to see me.

He helped me secure my first job as a security guard by night in the port and organised a place for me to stay before I got my own. Toni was really a good man underneath it all. I managed to go once every couple of months to see my uncle and his family and give them whatever I could spare. I visited Fat Toni every time I got a chance and after couple of years, he came to the port one day with a mixture of some terrible but also good news.

"Salem, my friend, my wife is very sick and she wants to go back home to die there. I'm selling my business and moving back to Italy. That's not the only reason why I'm here. I've received a letter from Signora Rossi and she mentioned you and asked that if you ever came about, I have to give you her address." Signore Maltese handed me the address and said farewell. I wished him luck and offered him my prayers for his sick wife.

"Thank you, Signore Maltese, for all your help."

"It was my pleasure, Salem. You take care now, si?"

"I will," I shouted back as he walked away and that was the last time I heard from or saw Signore Maltese. Truly he was a good, man but my promise to Signora Rossi had to wait for a few decades.

Eventually it was fulfilled in 1955, just a few years after Libya gained its independence. I had done well for myself. I got married and had two beautiful children: a boy and a girl. At that time, the Libyan Government made great efforts with the help of the new Italy to find out what exactly happened to those who vanished inside the concentration camps and in exile in those black days of terror. It was a promise I made to myself that I would not rest until I found out what became of my sister,

Aisha, the night she was snatched from our tent. The screams of those young girls still haunts me. It was a promise I made and now was the time to fulfil my promise.

I did my initial investigation in Benghazi and searched through all the archives that the Italians left behind after their heavy defeat in the Second World War, but there was nothing. So I set sail to Italy just a few days after the Christian New Year. The ship docked in the port of the city of Napoli. There I stayed for one night only before I took the train to Rome. It was a magnificent city. In Rome you smell history. I must say that I loved Rome from the moment my foot stepped onto the platform. I did not feel a stranger as my Italian was perfect. I knew how to deal with the Italians and most of all, I did not really look different to the average Italian male.

The city was buzzing and full of life. Immediately I set out finding a place to stay and could not resist going straight to the "Milano Hotel", which had some exquisite décor. When I was filling out the resident sheet, I noticed the elegant lady behind the counter began taking an interest in me the minute she spotted that I was from Libya.

"*Buonasera, signore.*" Then she took the sheet that I had just filled in and said, "Yes, Signore Bu–Ayesha, Salem Bu–Ayesha, you are very welcome to Italy. I hope you'll have a nice stay with us." She handed me the keys and asked the porter to show me the way. She was very elegant, sophisticated lady in her 60s, but she hid it very well. It was almost dinnertime when I arrived so I just freshened myself up and went downstairs to the restaurant. After dinner I went to the bar area where I ordered some coffee. I sat there for a while before I went out to discover the city of Rome. By the time I got back to my hotel, everybody was asleep except for the porter who opened the door to let me in.

The next morning I woke up quite early and had my breakfast. Then I performed my usual routine by moving to the bar area where I drunk my strong, black coffee and read my newspaper, contemplating how to start my quest.

A voice disturbed my reading and upon looking up, Signora Geroni was standing by my table. "*Buongiorno*, Signore Bu–

Ayesha. Forgive my intrusion. It's just strange, we don't see many Libyans in here. As a matter of fact, you're the first Libyan I've met."

"Sit down please. Can I order you something to drink, Signora Geroni?"

"No, *grazie mille*. I just wanted to have a chat that's all. I wanted to offer my help. If there is anything I can do for you, please ask." Signora Geroni was not only welcoming but generous as well. Of course, I did not have to think long. I took her offer seriously and before I knew it, I was telling her my whole story from the march to hell up to the day I said farewell to Signora Rossi. By the time I was finished, she was sobbing and very apologetic.

"We're not like that. We don't think of that past. We have put it behind us and moved on. The Fascist Italy is something we don't want to know." Signora Geroni vowed to help me and said, "I know the right man to do it." And that man was her husband, a retired general who fought alongside the Allies during the Second World War. Signora Geroni made the arrangements to meet here the following morning. I thanked her for her concern and for all her assistance.

At dawn, I woke up and got dressed. Soon I was at my usual place and ready to meet Signore Geroni. I ordered a coffee, sat down and read through the morning paper. I could not believe my eyes when I saw a small article about a former fascist general dying alone in hospital; General Rodolfo Graziani, the ruthless man who achieved his rank and medals by torturing innocent civilians. A man once named by the Il Duce himself as the "Pacifier of Cyrenaica", died alone and no one cared.

"There is justice afterall," I said to myself. The soft voice of Signora Geroni had snapped me out of my reverie as my mind had wandered while reading the article.

"*Buongiorno*, Signore Bu–Ayesha. How are you this morning?" she asked with big, cheerful smile on her face.

"*Buongiorno. Grazie mille*," I replied while getting up from my chair.

"This is my husband, Luka."

"*Come va*, Signore Geroni," I greeted while shaking hands with him.

"*Lo sto bene, grazie*, signore," he answered.

"It's very kind of you, sir, to come and see me. I really appreciate it very much. I am grateful."

"I am so glad to be here. My wife told me the whole story. I was shocked, I will help you, Signore Bu–Ayesha, with everything I can," Signore Geroni said with voice full assurance.

After we familiarised ourselves with one another, Signore Geroni suggested that we should start right away, as he explained to me that he made a few calls to certain places.

"We will go to these places, but please be prepared for some disappointment because it may prove difficult, if not impossible to find the people you seek, signore," he warned.

Moving around by car made things much easier. We visited at least five different places before finally arriving at the military archives, poring over the files of the period of the Italian occupation of Libya. Signore Geroni suggested we begin with the Cyrenaica division. Everyone there was more than helpful. They were so warm, cordial and sympathetic. They used every single trick they knew to track down information but there was nothing there to start with.

In the end and after a much needed cup of tea, I thanked them all for their sympathy and assistance in seeking the information we sought. Sidi Rajab's words after the snatching of Aisha rung in my ears, "Remember, Salem, that criminals always hide the evidence of their crime." I always wondered if Sidi Rajab knew something but could not say it then. I guess maybe he wanted me to live in hope or wanted me to find out for myself. I knew one thing that even though the news could be hard, it was the only way for my soul to have peace.

When we came back, Signora Geroni was there to receive us with open arms, but she was saddened by the outcome. Both she and her husband invited me to dinner at their house the following night. I had a wonderful time there. There was nothing left for me to do except fulfil the promise I made to Signora Rossi. Signora Geroni woke me up earlier than the usual time. By the time I got downstairs, Signora Geroni and her husband greeted me.

"Good morning, Salem. Listen, we know how much Signora Rossi means to you so we got you a return train ticket to Milano. It's the least we could do. Please accept it as a token of friendship and a way of saying sorry for what happened to you and your country."

I was truly shocked by their unbelievable gesture of generosity. "*Grazie, molte grazie.* You have done more than enough for me."

Once I had eaten and packed my bag, Signore Geroni drove me to the Stazione di Roma Centrale. While there, he explained how to get to Signora Rossi's village and he said that I should be fine from there. I took my seat by the window and began thinking of everything. I missed my wife and my children and could not wait to return to them.

The excitement of meeting Signora Rossi once again was indescribable. My heart was thumping rapidly. The train started moving slowly, leaving the majestic Rome behind. It gathered speed and momentum. The green hills, meadows, fields and valleys soon appeared on both sides of the train. The movement of the train on the rails made me close my eyes and before I knew it, I was asleep. I dreamt of Signora Rossi and Signora Rossellini, and in the dream they were as beautiful and young as ever.

I woke up a short distance from the Stazione di Milano Centrale. Milano was its last stop and Milano is another amazing city. I did not wish to waste any time wandering around, and commenced my journey to Signora Rossi's house. The bus station was not far and I purchased my ticket. I had another hour to spare before its departure so I visited the shops and bought Signora Rossi a little present, and also a newspaper to read in the bus. My destination was Grumello. The bus driver sounded the horn couple of times before moving off. The roads and scenery were a big contrast to what I had seen earlier.

"Bergamo. We will stop here for half an hour. So for those who are continuing the journey with us, do not drift away from the bus stop. There are a lot of cafés and places to eat. Please come back in half an hour. Enjoy," the driver said.

Bergamo, the city in the mountain, was a medieval town with lots of history behind it and looked like it was worth spending some time at. We boarded the bus once again and soon we were on the road. I asked the driver to give me a shout when we are in Grumello.

"*Signore, questa e la tua destinazione!*" the driver shouted before the bus came to a halt almost an hour later. I gathered my bag and newspaper and moved toward the front door.

"*Grazie mille*, signore for the enjoyable drive."

"*Grazie, mille. Buona fortuna*," the driver replied, honking the horn three times before departing.

It had been 23 years since I kissed Signora Rossi goodbye and I was here in the birthplace of the lady I came to see. It was very old village as I noticed the castle and medieval style buildings. It was just before sunset when I got there and a bit of a chill lingered in the air. I glanced around and it was very quiet. A bar was across the road so I went there for a cup of coffee and a little rest and to freshened up before going to see Signora Rossi. While there, I also intended to get some information in how to find Signora Rossi's place.

As soon as I pushed open the door, the smell of alcohol and a heavy cloud of smoke hit me. Once inside, all the locals turned their heads to see who had arrived. Soon they realised that I was a stranger, but the place possessed a warm and friendly feeling to it. I went straight to the counter and dropped my bag.

"*Buonasera, signore. Posso avera tazza di café per favour?*" I asked.

"*Buonasera.* You certainly are not from around here otherwise you would be ordering alcohol," the man said while smiling.

"*Si*, signore. I come from a faraway place," I replied. All the punters were looking and listening to the conversation.

"You must be Sicilian," the man behind the counter incorrectly surmised.

"No, sir, I am from Libya," I informed him. A bout of excited whispering and loud talk commenced.

"Paolo, get him a drink on me," one man said.

"We will all buy him a drink," added another.

"Grazie mille, gentlemen. I am only here for a few minutes. I thank you for your hospitality, but all I need is a cup of coffee, that's all."

"Okay, it's on the house," the bartender said while serving me the coffee. Most of the crowd seemed to be farmers, judging by the way they were dressed.

"So what brought you here to Grumello, signore, if you don't mind me asking?" the barman asked.

"No, not at all. I am here to visit someone very dear to me."

"Hey, this is something guys. Here is a man from Libya, coming to visit someone very dear to him from our town and we don't know about it! There's something wrong here," one punter commented while making all the others laugh.

"Who is it you're visiting? Forgive me, I am not trying to be nosey but maybe we can help you," the barman said.

"I am looking for Signora Rossi."

"You mean *the* Signora Rossi, Signora Allegra Rossi?"

"*Si*, signore. Signora Allegra Rossi," I confirmed.

"She is true lady and has done very well for herself. She's the most respected woman in the whole region. Most of the villagers work for her in some form or another. You also came at the right time as she's giving her daughter away today. The wedding is actually taking place in Signora Ross's house," the barman said. I was so delighted to hear the news for both Signora Rossi and Sofia. Then the men asked how and where did I get to know her? I briefly told them my story. Much like every other Italian I had met, they were all sympathetic toward me.

"Well, signore, you're in good hands. We will get you to Signora Rossi's place as soon as you ready," the barman assured me.

"In a couple of minutes, if that's okay with you? I want to get there before dark." I had to fix myself and comb my hair.

I looked rather well as I bought a suit from Napoli for this occasion.

Once I got back from the toilet, some men stood up and the barman shouted, "Marco, take the man to Signora Rossi's place and I'll have something for you when you get back."

I said goodbye to them and promised that I would return before going home. Marco drove an old and battered car that probably bought during the First World War, as I could not figure out its make. Marco and I talked for a little while as the car began navigating its way through narrow roads.

"This is Signora Rossi's place. I can't go any further. It's better if you walk as I don't want to disturb anything," Marco said. "It's a nice walk to the main house. You will enjoy it," Marco added while getting a cigarette from his cigarette case.

"*Grazie, molte grazie.* I will see you before I go. I owe you one," I replied while getting out of the car.

"*Arrivaderci, buona fortuna.*" Marco waved and then pulled off.

"I will need it, Marco. *Arrivederci,*" I replied. Now I was alone, standing outside a big wooden gate. There were lots of balloons of different colours attached to the gate and its pillars. I checked myself for the last time and I made my way through the gate. There were big trees on both sides of the road. The branches of the trees of each side tangled together making the road look like a tunnel. The sun was sinking in the horizon giving everything a sort of orangey colour.

It was really weird. When I left Signora Rossi, I was nearly 10, a young kid and she was a woman in her prime. She was in her 40s back then and now I was a young man and Signora Rossi was hitting 70.

"Such is the circle of life," I told myself. After trekking up the long path, her house soon began appearing. It was a mansion, the different types of noises and sounds assailing my ears grew louder as I got closer. Then I saw the crowd. There were many people all smartly dressed. A band was playing and children ran around the place. There were lights everywhere and people were dancing. Large tables containing food and drinks. But my eyes were searching for one person.

Upon nearing her doorstep, my heart pulsated faster and my legs became weak. I was spotted by the children first as I heard them saying, "There is someone coming." At that time I thought everyone was looking toward me. I thought the music had stopped and people became silent. I could see Signora Rossi sitting on a white chair next to other ladies. She had aged but still retained that beautiful, amiable face.

I walked through the crowd and walked toward her. When I was a few metres from where she was sitting, I stopped. Signora Rossi looked at me and then she gently stood up. We walked towards to each other and she held my arms and I, hold hers. Everyone was clueless as to what was occurring.

"Signora Rossi, I am glad I have found you alive and well," I said with tears threatening to fall.

"Salem, my sweetheart. You came! Look at you, you're a handsome devil. I always knew you'd be a fine looking man," Signora Rossi said also teary-eyed. We hugged, talked and embraced once more. We both cried and laughed some more before embracing each other again.

Then Sofia and Alexander joined in the proceedings.

"We know who you are. You're the legendary Salem," some children said. "Aunt Allegra mentioned you all the time in her fairytales to us."

I did not want to take the attention away from Sofia so I quickly took Signora Rossi and danced with her all night long. As the night progressed, it grew colder so we all moved inside the house. Signora Rossi took us to a large room with a big open fireplace. We sat by the fire and chatted well into the night . Because it was so late, Signora Rossi was getting tired and I got Sofia to take her to her room. Alexander and I sat for a little while and talked first about the ghost, about Formaggio, and then about our life after we went separate ways. He went on to become a doctor and lived in Milano. After our discussion, a made was escorting me to the guest room but was unable to sleep due to the excitement.

The next morning, Sofia and her husband said goodbye before they drove to their honeymoon in Venice. All the relations and the immediate family had left in the afternoon. Signora Rossi took me for a walk around the farm and she showed me her horses. That night we had a relaxing, quiet dinner. Signora Rossi told me about her husband and how he wanted to go to Ethiopia and take them with him but she refused to repeat the same mistake. He was looking for glory gained by depriving others of their freedom. She told him that she could not be part of it and left him, taking the children with her. Signora Rossi returned home where she invested the money she made back in Libya and made a good profit. With some money in her pockets, she bought some land and then sold it when things got better.

"I told him that we'd always be here for him when he gets back, but he never did come back," she said. I detected a sense of sadness in her voice. "News came one day that he died in the battlefield. Like the old saying goes, Salem, 'you live by the sword, you die by the sword'."

"I'm so sorry, Allegra."

"It's okay, Salem. There's no need to be. I don't regret the decision. I'm much happier here." She apologised once again for the suffering my country endured at the hands of the Italian invaders. "Signora Rossellini left her husband for Dawoud. She got him citizenship and brought him to Italy, but she could not live in peace because the whole family turned their backs on her and never accepted him. They eventually emigrated to America. The last time I heard from them, she told me that they were very happy there and promised to keep in touch. Signora Rossellini wanted to come to the wedding but was unable to make arrangements." Signora Rossi paused for a few seconds and wiped a tear from her eye. "She always loved you, Salem. My friend always believed that there was something special about you."

I gave her a little present and she gave me something in return for the children. Signora Rossi and I gazed at the stars until daybreak. By the afternoon, I was getting ready to get to the village to catch my bus to Milano and then to Rome. Signora Rossi gave me an envelope and made me promise not to open it until my ship was in the middle of the sea. She held me in a tight embrace and then kissed me on the cheek before bidding farewell. That was the last time I saw Signora Rossi. We kept in touch by mail for 15 years and then sadly, the letters stopped. I kept writing for a while before finally deciding to no longer write to her. I doubt that anyone would have ever understood the bond between us. Even Sofia, Alexander and Signore Rossi could not comprehend it.

Signora Rossi's driver brought me to the village. I had time to buy those men a drink before taking my bus toward the long journey home. In Rome I stayed an extra night and spent most of it chatting with Signora and Signore Geroni. I thanked them dearly and continued my journey.

While the ship was at sea and as Napoli began disappearing, I took the envelope that Signora Rossi gave me and went upstairs to the deck. I sat down as the sun descended slowly. I opened Signora Rossi's envelope and was shocked to find a respectable amount of money along with a letter. It read:

Dearest Salem,

When you open this letter, you will be heading home and thinking of yesterday. I will pray to the Lord that he will give you the strength so you can forgive my country for its wrongdoings. I am desperate for your forgiveness. When you came into my life, you gave me peace and because of you, I became a nicer person. Now I want you to have peace because your soul will never rest until you come to know the truth about Aisha and those young girls. I am also praying to God to have mercy upon us. I want you to know that Aisha and the young girls never made it outside Al-agaila. They were brutally raped and then killed. My husband told me a long time ago but I didn't think it was fair to tell you then. I know that you are suffering right now, and as horrible as I feel about myself, I have an obligation to tell you. I am so sorry for what happened to you and I know you will rise with your soul above those who hurt you because when I met you, I was crumbling and you made me stronger. Please, I ask you never try to forget me, but I beg you try to forgive not only me, but also my country. I hope that you will have peace. I will pray for you until I am no longer in this world.

I love you with all my heart.

Allegra.

P. S. What's in the envelope is not a gift; it's money you earned. I was just waiting for the right time to give it to you. I hope it will be of some help to you and your family.

I cried during the whole time I read that letter. I read it again and again until I felt that my heart was cleansed of grief. I learned that we must wash our hearts with tears or eventually it will rust.

From my time on this earth, I have learned that there are no winners in wars because we all as the citizens of this planet have to nurse the scars that remain from such wars. I also learned that the healing process takes a long time. In wars there's nothing but destruction, sadness, and in my case, orphaned children. As for me, I have learned to forgive but not to forget. I have learned to cope with my pain because that is all one can really do.

* * *

Dublin, 2009

The salty smell originating from the sea wafted past my nose. My father's voice started fading away, there were tears in my eyes and even more clouds blanketed the sky. The wind gathered momentum once again and rain started falling.

BIBLIOGRAPHY/REFERENCES

The Archives of the Italian Military Courts in Libya. A publication of the Libyan centre of study for the Libyan resistance against the Italian invasion. 1991. Part 1, 2, and 3.

A Libyan hero (1862–1931) The pnblication of Libya our home, Dr Ebraheem Egnaywa.

Rodolfo Graziani – Pace Romanin Libia. Roma, 1937.

Libyans in Exile From the Direct Cause of the Colonial Italian Invasion (Libya, 1987)

Abu–Alasha, Farag Omar Al-Mukhtar – TheAarticles, Libya Our Home.

The Italian Occupation and the Libyan Resistance. Libya Our Home.

Omar Al-Mukhtar, the publication of the centre of study of the Libyan resistance against the Italian invasion of Libya.

Ahmed Albouri, Dr. Wahbi Benghazi Society in the First Half of the Twentieth Century. The House of the National Books. Libya 2008.

Dinolfo, Innio Mussollini la Politica Estera Italiana 1919–1933 (Padova, 1960).

Rochat, Giorgio Al Repressione Della Resistenza Arabian Cirenaica Genna (Marzo 1973).

Rava, Carlo Emilio Al Margini Del Sahara (Bologna, 1936)

Rochat, Giorgio La Repressione Della Resistenza In Cirenaica.

Geroni, Cioanni Spigolature Bengasine (Fireenza, 1913).

R. Smith, Denis Le Guerre Del Duce (Roma, 1976)

Maltese, Paolo La Terra Roma Essa (Monadadori, 1974).

Del Caseini, Mario Mussolini Africa (Mantova, 1926).

Graziani, Rodolfo Hdifeso Lpatria (Milano, 1948).

Volpi, Giuseppe La Politica Coloniale Del Fascismo (Milano, 1929)

Delboca, Angelo Gu Italine In Libia (Roma– Bari, 1986).

Nasi, Guglieimo Laguerra In Libia Rivesta Militari Genn (Roma 1927).

Defelice, Renzo Ebrei Un Paese Arabo (Bologna, 1973).

Brezzi, G. Contogiorni Di Prigionia Nelloasi Di Kufra (Milano, 1930).